Witch Is How Berries Tasted Good

Published by Implode Publishing Ltd
© Implode Publishing Ltd 2018

The right of Adele Abbott to be identified as the Author of the Work has been asserted by her in accordance with the Copyright, Designs and Patents Act 1988.

All rights reserved, worldwide.
No part of this publication may be reproduced, stored in a retrieval system, or transmitted, in any form or by any means without the prior written permission of the copyright owner.

The characters and events in this book are fictitious. Any similarity to real persons, dead or alive, is purely coincidental and not intended by the author.

Chapter 1

"I don't believe it!" Jack thumped the dashboard, and tried the ignition again, but without success.

"What's wrong with it?" I said.

"How should I know?"

"Okay. There's no need to bite my head off."

"Sorry. I'm just tired. I'd better call the breakdown service, but goodness knows how long they'll be at this time of night."

The good news was they weren't very long at all.

But then, the bad news.

"The starter motor's blown," said the altogether too cheery mechanic.

"Can't you just put a new one on?" I said.

"Sorry, love, but we can't carry parts for every make of car, and there's nowhere open at—." He checked his watch. "Two-thirty in the morning. Have you guys just got back from holiday?"

"Honeymoon," Jack said.

"Nice." He gave us what I assumed was a knowing wink. "It's a pity you had to come back to this."

"What happens now?" My patience was wearing thin.

"You have the comprehensive plan, so I can tow you to the nearest garage, or I can take you back to your house. Whichever you'd prefer."

"Take us home."

Roger, that was his name, gave us a blow-by-blow account of his and Eileen's honeymoon in Clacton-on-Sea, and he didn't spare any of the details. More's the pity.

"There you go." He'd left the stricken car on the road outside our house. "Have a happy married life."

"Thanks very much." Jack stuffed a fiver into the man's hand.

"Cheers, buddy."

"Why did you give him a tip?" I said, once Roger had driven away.

"Why not?"

"He should have paid us for having to listen to his sordid honeymoon stories."

"I thought he was okay. Come on, we should try to get some sleep."

We grabbed our suitcases from the car and headed for the house. I couldn't wait to put my head on the pillow.

"What the—?" Jack stopped dead in his tracks, just inside the door.

"What's wrong now?" I stepped into the hall.

"Duck!" He called out as the coffee table came floating past my head. "Get down on the floor."

I didn't need telling twice.

"What's going on, Jill?"

"Why are you asking me?"

"Our furniture is floating around the house. Call me crazy, but I'm guessing that magic is involved."

"Madge must have done it."

Under pressure from Grandma, I'd agreed to let her friend, Madge Moleworthy, stay at our house while we were on honeymoon.

"Can't you stop it?" Jack ducked to avoid a vase.

"I could."

"What are you waiting for, then?" Jack had to duck even lower to avoid a low-flying magazine rack.

"If I reverse the spell now, all the furniture will fall to the floor wherever it happens to be." I pointed to the open lounge door. "The bedside cabinet is in there."

"What other option do we have?"

"None I guess." So I reversed the spell, and all the furniture fell to the floor. The sound was deafening.

"Why would Madge have done this?" Jack said when we were back on our feet.

"I've no idea, but I'm going to have a few choice words to say to her tomorrow."

"It'll take us ages to get everything back into the right rooms. Can't you just cast a spell to do it?"

"You mean the good old *put-the-furniture-back-in-the-right-room* spell?"

"That sounds like it would work."

"It probably would — if it actually existed, but it doesn't. The only way we're going to get everything back to where it should be is to move it ourselves."

"We'll be up all night doing that."

"I won't. I'm going to bed. This lot will have to wait until the morning."

"Where is the bed, anyway?"

"Oh no, please don't tell me—" I rushed upstairs. "It's okay. It's still in the bedroom. It's too large to float out of the door."

Jack followed me up. "I'll have to call in to work in the morning, to tell them I'll be late."

"You can't mention the furniture."

"Give me some credit. I'll just tell them I have to wait to get the car repaired."

***

"Someone's at the door." Jack nudged me awake.

"What time is it?"

"Don't know." He put the pillow over his head.

"I grabbed my phone from the bedside table. It was eight-thirty. We'd been in bed for less than four hours.

Whoever was at the door knocked again.

"Can't you get it?" I poked Jack in his side, but he just snored in response. "Great! I guess I'll do it then."

I threw on my dressing gown and manoeuvred my way through the labyrinth of errant furniture.

"Welcome home, Mrs Maxwell."

"Kathy? What are you doing here?"

"Pete's working in Smallwash today, so I thought I'd—" She looked past me. "Why are the dining room chairs in the hall?"

"I—err—"

Without waiting to be invited, she stepped inside.

"And why is the washing basket in the lounge?"

"Err—I—err—" I turned to the stairs. "Jack! Kathy's here. Come and say hello."

"There was no need to wake him," she said.

"It's okay. He was just about to get up anyway."

"What's up?" Jack appeared at the top of the stairs, looking like death warmed up. "Oh. Hi, Kathy."

"Morning, Jack." She grinned. "Still recovering from the honeymoon?"

"Kathy was just asking about the furniture," I said. "I was about to tell her that moving the furniture around was all your idea, but now you're here, you can explain it yourself. I'll go and put the kettle on."

I didn't hurry making the tea because I wanted to give Jack ample time to explain the furniture situation. When I eventually went through to the lounge, the coffee table was nowhere to be seen, so I handed their drinks to them.

"Has Jack told you what we've been up to?" I said.

"Err—yeah, kind of. I'm just not sure I buy this Feng Shui stuff. And anyway, I thought it just involved moving things around in the same room. I didn't think you had to move stuff from one room to another."

I was impressed by Jack's quick thinking, and I played along. "You're talking about conventional Feng Shui. This is ultimate Feng Shui. Very different."

"Right, well, whatever floats your boat."

Or furniture.

"Shouldn't you be opening the shop soon, Kathy?"

"Nope. I don't need to be there until ten."

"How come?"

"While you were away, I took on a part-time assistant, May Knott. She's going to do a few hours each week."

"She doesn't sound very reliable."

"What do you mean?"

"Well, she *may not* show up. Get it? May Knott—may not."

Kathy and Jack both groaned.

"What do you think of the garden?" Kathy said.

"What do you mean?"

"Haven't you seen it? Pete took out the sandpit while you were away."

"It was dark when we got home last night, so we went straight to bed. As soon as we'd finished with the Feng Shui, that is."

"Let's take a look." Jack led the way through to the

kitchen.

"Why is there an armchair in here?" Kathy shook her head.

"You can't argue with ultimate Feng Shui."

"The garden looks great." Jack got to the window first. "Peter's done a fantastic job. Are you sure we don't owe him anything, Kathy?"

"Positive. We thought it was better than getting you yet another toaster." She glanced around. "Speaking of which—where is your toaster?"

"In the back bedroom, I think."

"Right." She rolled her eyes. "So, what do *you* think of the garden, Jill?"

"It's fantastic. It looks so much bigger now that the sandpit has gone. Thanks."

After Kathy had left, Jack showered and dressed, and then dealt with the mechanic who came from the local garage to collect the car. We then spent the next two hours moving all the furniture back to its correct location. By the time we were done, I was exhausted.

"I can give you a lift to West Chipping if you like," I offered.

"There's no need. Just drop me at the station. The trains are pretty much every fifteen minutes."

"Well done on the Feng Shui explanation, by the way. I was impressed."

"Thanks, but how will we explain to Kathy why we've moved all the furniture back, the next time she comes over?"

"You'll think of something."

***

I dropped Jack at the station, and then parked in my usual spot in the city centre. As I was walking to the office, my phone rang.

"Jill. It's Madge Moleworthy."

"Madge? What on earth happened at the house?"

"I'm so sorry."

"It took us ages to move all the furniture back. What were you thinking?"

"I didn't do it, but it was still entirely my fault."

"Who did do it?"

"My cousin, Martha. She and I have been playing practical jokes on one another ever since we were kids. While I was over here, I turned her tap water into strawberry soda. It was hilarious."

"It sounds it." Not.

"Anyway, Martha decided to get her own back on me. She must have come over to your house in the night and cast the 'float' spell. She'd assumed I'd be in bed, but I'd already left for home. I didn't know anything about it until she rang me this morning. How bad was it?"

"Bad enough."

"I really am sorry, Jill. Is there anything I can do to make it up to you?"

"It's alright. Everything's back to normal now. Anyway, I have to get going. I'm just on my way into the office."

"Okay. Sorry again."

I was really looking forward to seeing the new sign: Jill Maxwell – Private Investigator. Hopefully, Sid Song had kept his promise and installed it while we were away.

He had. I could see it — wait a minute! What the — ?

I hurried up the stairs and found Mrs V hard at work on her tapestry.

"Welcome back, Jill. How was the honeymoon?"

"Very nice, thanks."

"I hope you took lots of photos."

"Quite a few, yeah. Look, about the — "

"And the photos from the wedding? Have you got those yet?"

"Not yet, no. What happened with — "

"The sign? You noticed it, then?"

"I could hardly miss it. Why does it say: Gooder and Maxwell?"

"I don't know, dear."

"Why didn't you stop them from putting it up?"

"I wasn't here. My sister had another one of her funny turns, so I had to go down there to see her. When I came in the next day, it was already up."

"Have you spoken to Sid Song?"

"Of course. I rang him straight away, and he admitted that it's his fault. He said he'll change it free of charge."

"I should think so too. When's he bringing the new one?"

"Hmm. There's a slight problem there."

"What kind of problem?"

"Mr Song rang me the next day. Apparently, he'd been at a meeting of his barbershop choir when he fell and sprained his ankle. He said it may be a while before he can replace the sign."

"Great! That's just great."

"I'm really sorry, Jill."

"It isn't your fault. How is your sister, anyway?"

"She's fine. She was over-reacting as usual."

"I see you're still working on the tapestry. It doesn't seem to have grown much since I was last here."

"It's way more fiddly than I expected." She handed it to me. "What do you think of it so far?"

"It's looking good. That figure there is obviously you."

"You're right. It is."

"And that figure of you is knitting something." I squinted to get a better look. "Oh, I see. The figure of you in the tapestry is knitting a tapestry. That's very good." I moved it even closer to my eyes. "Wait a minute. Doesn't that figure also have a figure of you, knitting a tapestry?"

"That's right, dear."

No wonder it was taking her so long. It was the tapestry equivalent of Russian dolls. How she'd managed to include such detail was nothing short of a miracle.

"How's Winky been? I hope you remembered to feed him."

"Of course I did, but I'm glad you're back. I hate going home, smelling of cat."

"Winky doesn't smell."

"Hmm. Speaking of which, I hope you complained to the hotel."

"What about?"

"The smell of cat. You must have noticed it at the ceremony and again at the reception."

"Err—no, I can't say I did."

"Quite a few people mentioned it. You should definitely ask for some kind of compensation."

"Right, well, I'd better make a start."

I thought Winky would be pleased to see me because it

meant he wouldn't have to put up with Mrs V any longer, but he didn't even glance up from the computer screen.

"I'm back."

"So I see." He was typing, frantically.

"You know you're not supposed to use my computer."

"Shush! Can't you see I'm busy?"

Charming.

I walked across to my desk and peered over his head at the screen.

"What's that you're doing?"

"It's my new business venture."

"Another one? What is it this time?"

"I'm now a fully-fledged Feng Shui consultant."

"Please tell me you're joking."

"I'm deadly serious. After I heard how much the old bag lady had paid to get someone to move her furniture around, I figured there were big bucks to be made. And I was right."

"Who's going to take Feng Shui advice from a cat?"

"That's the clever part. My consultations are provided online, so no one knows they're dealing with a feline. Look." He pointed at the screen. "This software creates images of all the furniture in a room. I just use the mouse to move stuff around on-screen. The client then follows the plan to re-arrange the furniture."

"So, you get the client to do all the heavy lifting themselves?"

"That's right."

"And how do you decide where to position the furniture?"

"I spend hours consulting the Feng Shui instruction manual."

"Really?"

"Of course not." He laughed. "I just shuffle them around at random."

"And how much do you charge for that?"

"I'm able to offer budget prices because I don't actually have to pay site visits. One hundred pounds per room on average."

"And how long does it take you per room?"

"Five minutes max."

"Unbelievable."

"So, you can see why I'm going to need your computer for the foreseeable future."

"What am I supposed to do?"

"For a start, you could get that stupid sign changed. Gooder and Maxwell? It makes you sound like a vaudeville act. Anyway, how was the honeymoon? I want all the sordid details."

"Never you mind about my honeymoon—how's your love life coming along?"

"It isn't. They've all dumped me."

"What? Trixie, Judy and—"

"Daisy. Yeah. They found out about one another and turned up here en masse."

"I wish I'd been here to see that."

"It wasn't pretty. Anyway, who cares? It's their collective loss. When I make a million from Budget Feng Shui Online, they'll be sorry. That reminds me. I'll need you to give me a lift across town on Friday."

"Why? What's happening then?"

"I'm going to speed-dating."

I laughed.

"What's so funny?"

"Speed dating for cats? I assume you're joking."

"No, I'm not. I'll have you know that felines were speed dating long before you two-leggeds came up with the idea."

"I don't have time to chauffeur you around."

"You owe me for what you did to me at the wedding. I still haven't got over that."

"Do you plan to guilt trip me about that forever?"

"Probably."

Chapter 2

After a little gentle persuasion (red not pink), I eventually managed to convince Winky that he should let me get to my desk and computer. When I sat down, I spotted the note I'd left for myself before I went away on honeymoon: Consult with Grandma, re marketing.

After the start to the day I'd just had, the last thing I wanted to do was go cap in hand to Grandma, but it had to be done. Luther had made it quite clear that if I didn't increase my turnover and profitability soon, the business might go to the wall. The thought of having to look for a job was even less appealing than having to ask Grandma for help. The only bosses I'd ever had were my dad and myself. I wasn't sure I'd do well working for someone else.

To my surprise, she answered on the first ring.

"Yes?"

"It's me, Grandma."

"I know that. Your name is right there on the screen in front of me."

"I'm back from honeymoon."

"And you rang to tell me that? Unlike you, I don't have time for idle chit chat. I have a new product to launch."

"What's that?"

"The anti-ageing cream. I told you all about it."

"Right. I remember now."

"So? What do you want?"

"I need your help."

"With what? Are you fed up with that human of yours already? Do you want me to dispose of him for you? I could do it very discreetly."

"No, of course not. Jack and I are very much in love."
"What is it then? Hurry up."
"Business hasn't been great lately, so—"
"You want a job. Why didn't you say so?"
"No, I don't want a job. I wondered if you could help with my marketing? I have to try and pull in some new clients."
"What's in it for me?"
"The satisfaction of helping your granddaughter?"
"No, seriously." She cackled. "What's in it for me?"
"I don't know. What do you want? I can't afford to pay you."
"How about twenty percent of all the new business I help to generate?"
"How about five percent?"
"Ten."
"Okay, ten."
"Right, bye."
"Hold on, Grandma. When do we start?"
"I'll be in touch."
The line went dead.

***

The wailing sound made Winky's ears prick up. "What's that?"
"No idea." The noise seemed to be coming from the outer office, so I went to investigate. "Mrs V? What's wrong?"
She was in floods of tears, and it was several minutes before she was able to speak.
"I'm sorry, Jill."

"There's no need to apologise. Just tell me what's the matter."

"I've just heard that one of my oldest friends, Pat Volkes, has died. We've known one another since we were children."

"I'm so sorry. Was it expected?"

"Not really. I mean, she was getting on in years, but aren't we all?"

We?

Mrs V continued, "She was in reasonable health. At least, I thought so."

"If you'd like to go home—"

"No, but I will need to take time off for the funeral. It's next week."

"Of course. Did she have family?"

"Just a daughter, but she lives in Wales. It's only a couple of months since Pat moved into a care home. She did it as much for the company as anything else."

"Are you sure you wouldn't like to go home?"

"No, I'm okay now. It just came as a bit of a shock, that's all."

"I'll make us both a cup of tea, shall I?"

"That would be nice. Thank you, dear."

"What was that noise?" Winky said. "If it's another cat, I'll sort it out."

"It wasn't a cat. It was Mrs V."

"What on earth is wrong with her?"

"She's just heard that a friend of hers has died."

"At her age, she must be used to that. She's only just hanging on by a thread herself."

"Your compassion astounds me."

"Coming from you, that's pretty rich."

"I'll have you know that I'm full of compassion."

"You're full of something, but it doesn't smell much like compassion to me."

I'd enjoyed the honeymoon, but there had been one major problem: no custard creams.

Luckily, Mrs V had thought to buy a new packet ready for my return.

"How many would you like, Jill?"

"Err — you can just leave the packet."

"Are you sure that's wise? Can you trust yourself?"

"Of course. Self-restraint is my middle name."

Just then, someone called from the outer office, "Hello!"

While Mrs V went to check who the visitor was, I slipped the packet of biscuits into the top drawer of my desk. Just for safe keeping, obviously.

"There's a Mrs Shuttlebug to see you. She said she dropped in on the off-chance that you could see her."

"Show her in, please."

"Before I do, I should have mentioned earlier that I've booked an appointment for you this afternoon. It's a Mr and Mrs Banks at two o'clock. I hope that's okay."

"That's fine."

"Deloris, this is a surprise."

"Hello, Jill. I hope you don't mind my just dropping in like this. I wanted to share my good news with you."

"Take a seat."

"I found out on Friday that Cuthbert's book is going to be published."

"Really? That's fantastic."

"And it's all thanks to you. The story about the aurochilla made all the newspapers in Candlefield. It was even picked up by radio and TV. Not long after that, I was contacted by two different publishers who were both interested in acquiring the rights to Cuthbert's work."

"Have you decided which one you'll go with?"

"Actually, I was also approached by a literary agent. She came to see me—a very nice lady by the name of Brenda Badstorm. I signed with her, and she handled the negotiations for the book. We agreed a deal with a publisher on Friday."

"I'm so pleased for you."

"Cuthbert would have been thrilled."

"Do you ever hear from him?"

"Sorry? Oh, I see what you mean. No. He and I discussed the matter many times, and we agreed that we'd bypass Ghost Town. He won't find out about the book until I join him, and I'm not planning on doing that just yet. It'll be a nice surprise for him when I do."

"I trust your agent negotiated a good deal for you?"

"I think so. It's certainly much more than my pension pays. I'd like to give you something, Jill. By way of a thank you."

"That's really not necessary."

"I thought you might like a first edition when it's published. Even if you don't read it, it'll make a nice coffee table book."

"That's very kind. I'd like that."

"Great." She stood up. "I won't take up any more of your time. I'm sure you're busy. I'm going to spend the rest of the day shopping, by way of celebration. It's not often I come to the human world."

"You should have asked for a cut of the royalties," Winky said, after Deloris had left.

"There's more to life than money."

"You've changed your tune. Married life has made you soft."

***

Monday was Aunt Lucy's day off from babysitting, so I thought I'd pay her a visit while it was quiet over there.

Best laid plans, and all that.

Amber, Pearl and the babies were all there.

"Jill!" Amber gave me a hug. "How was the honeymoon?"

"Do you have photos?" Pearl said.

"The honeymoon was great, thanks. Jack took some photos with his digital camera. I'll copy them onto my phone before the next time I come over."

"Morning, Jill," Aunt Lucy called from the sofa. She had the babies on either side of her.

"I thought Monday was your day off?"

"So did I." She grinned.

"We don't like to think of Mum being all alone in this house." Amber picked up a soft toy.

"That's right," Pearl said. "We thought she'd like the company."

"How very selfless of the two of you. By the way, what do I call the little ones now?"

"Lily," Amber said.

"Lily," Pearl echoed.

"Come on, you two, this is ridiculous. You can't call

them both by the same name."

"I've been trying to tell them that." Aunt Lucy sounded exasperated. "Not that it's done any good."

"I decided on Lily first," Amber said.

"No, you didn't," Pearl countered.

This needed sorting out once and for all. "If you don't do something about it now, the two girls will be really confused when they're older. You both liked the name Lil, didn't you?"

They nodded.

"And you both like the name Lily?"

They nodded again.

"Right then. We just need to decide which one will be Lil and which one will be Lily."

"How are we supposed to do that?" Pearl said.

"Wait here." I went through to the kitchen where Aunt Lucy kept the notepad she used for her shopping lists. I scribbled the names on separate sheets of paper, folded them up, and returned to the lounge. "Okay. Who wants to pick first?"

"Me." Amber grabbed one.

Pearl took the other.

"Lily!" Pearl said.

"Lil." Amber smiled. "I always preferred that name, anyway."

"Thank goodness that's settled."

"Jill." Aunt Lucy got up from the sofa. "Why don't you come and sit with Lil and Lily while I go and make us all a nice cup of tea?"

"Okay." I took her place. "Now, which one is which?" I glanced from one baby to the other.

"That's Lil, obviously." Amber pointed to the baby on

my right. "She's the prettier one."

"She is not," Pearl said.

Oh boy.

"So, you two, have I missed anything while I've been away? No more brilliant new business initiatives, I hope?"

"No," Amber said. "After the disaster of the self-order machines, we're going to leave well alone."

"You are still using the machines though, aren't you?"

"Yeah, but hardly any of the customers bother with them. They were a complete waste of money."

***

I'd magicked myself back to Washbridge, and was walking to the office when I bumped into an old nemesis of mine: Dougal Andrews—The Bugle's *star* reporter.

Normally, I would have crossed the road to avoid him, but there was something about his demeanour that was different today, and curiosity got the better of me. When he spotted me walking towards him, he waved.

"Hello, Jill."

Something was definitely amiss.

"Are you alright, Dougal?"

"Not really. A reporter friend of mine was murdered recently."

"I'm sorry to hear that."

"Donna was one of the best."

Coming from Dougal Bugle, that was praise indeed. I'd always had him down as a male chauvinist pig.

"What happened?"

"She was killed in a hit-and-run in West Chipping."

"I thought you said she'd been *murdered*?"

"She was. There's no way that was an accident. Someone wanted her out of the way."

"Why?"

"She'd been working undercover on a story. I reckon someone must have realised she was a reporter."

"And murdered her? What was she working on?"

"I've no idea. No one knows. Donna was a freelance who's provided articles to The Bugle for years. She got to pick her own stories. The first anyone knew about them was when she brought the completed feature to the editor. That fellow of yours works out of West Chipping now, doesn't he?"

"Jack? Yeah."

"Look. I realise that you and I have never been drinking buddies, but have a word with him, would you? Tell him they need to take a closer look at what happened because it was no accident."

"Okay. I'll mention it to him tonight."

"Thanks."

***

Mr and Mrs Banks arrived at two on the dot. Middle-aged, there was a distinct air of sadness about them.

"I'm Gordon and this is my wife, Christine."

"Pleased to meet you both."

"Are you Gooder or Maxwell?" he asked.

"Err—both, actually. There was a little misunderstanding with the new sign. I used to be Jill Gooder until I got married two weeks ago. Now I'm Jill Maxwell."

"Is it just you here, then?" Christine said.

"Just me and the cat." I pointed to Winky who was curled up asleep on the sofa. "But he isn't much help to be honest."

Winky opened his one eye and gave me *that* look.

"We're here because our daughter, Annette, has gone missing," Gordon said.

"We're desperate," his wife interrupted. "Please say you'll help us."

"How long has she been missing?"

"Two weeks."

"What about the police? What have they done so far?"

"Absolutely nothing!" There was no mistaking the anger in his voice.

"That's rather unusual. Have they said why they haven't taken any action?"

"No, that's why we're here today. We can't just stand by and do nothing."

"Does your daughter normally live at home with you?"

"No. She shares a flat with a lovely young woman called Gaye."

"You've spoken to her, I assume?"

"Of course, but she has no more idea of what's happened than we do."

"Does Annette work?"

"No. She's a full-time student in her last year at college. We help her financially, so she doesn't have to take a part-time job."

"Boyfriend?"

"She did have one, but they split up a couple of months ago."

"Could that have been the reason for her disappearance? Was she upset at the split?"

"A little, but not enough to disappear without a word."
"Do you have a photo of Annette with you?"
Christine took one from her handbag and gave it to me.
"She's very pretty. Is it okay if I hang onto this?"
"Of course."

After Mr and Mrs Banks had left, I couldn't help but feel there was something they weren't telling me. The police are usually reluctant to consider an adult to be a missing person unless at least twenty-four hours has passed. But after two weeks, I could think of no good reason for the police not to have got involved. Maybe Jack would have some bright ideas.

***

When I arrived home, Tony and Clare, our next-door neighbours, were out front, and for the first time in weeks, they weren't dressed in costumes.
"Hello, you two. Don't you have a Con this weekend?"
"Hi, Jill." Clare managed only a weak smile. "We should be going to BearCon, which is one of our favourites, but I don't think we're going to make it."
"You both look a little peaky if you don't mind me saying."
"We're better now than we've been for a couple of days, but I'm not sure we'll be well enough to make it to the Con. It's a pity because we have some fabulous costumes. Mine is a panda, and Tony's is a polar bear."
"Have you had a virus?"
"No, at least, I don't think so. I reckon it was something we ate."

Jack arrived home just before six. "I've just bumped into Jimmy and Kimmy. They look terrible."

"Of course they do. Why would anyone want to dress up as a clown?"

"They weren't in costume. They were coming back from the corner shop. They both look quite ill, and they think it might be something they've eaten."

"That's weird. I saw Tony and Clare earlier, and they said exactly the same thing."

"How was your first day back at work?"

"Not great. They managed to get the sign wrong; it says Gooder and Maxwell."

"Catchy. I like it."

"I don't. Then I had to ask Grandma for help with my marketing."

"How did that go?"

"It was every bit as painful as you might expect. She wants ten percent of any new business she helps to bring in."

"That's family for you."

"I saw Dougal Andrews from The Bugle. One of his colleagues, Donna Lewis, was killed in a hit-and-run in West Chipping. Have you heard anything about it?"

"I saw some mention of it. The car was found burnt out some miles away."

"Dougal reckons it was deliberate. Donna was working undercover, and he thinks she may have upset the wrong person."

"What was she working on?"

"No one knows."

"It isn't much to go on, but I'll take a look at it

tomorrow."

"Thanks. Oh, and can you think of any reason why the police wouldn't get involved in a situation where a young woman has been missing for two weeks?"

"None. After that length of time, we're always going to get involved."

"That's what I thought."

Chapter 3

Jack and I were walking down the street when, all of a sudden, the pavement in front of us tipped into the air. We were thrown to the ground, and began to roll down the road towards the giant chasm that had opened up beneath us.

"Jill!" Jack shouted, as we continued to tumble. "Jill! Wake up!"

I opened my eyes to find that I was lying on the floor, next to the bed.

"What happened?"

"The bed's bust." He helped me up. "It must have been weakened when it fell to the floor after floating around."

The back leg of the bed had broken off, causing it to tip to one side.

"I thought it was a dream." I wiped the sleep from my eyes.

"A nightmare, more like. We'll have to fork out for a new one."

"Can't you just nail it back together?"

"Nails won't hold it, and besides, we were getting ready for a new bed."

"How did we manage to wear this one out so quickly?"

"Do you really need to ask?" He grinned. "Can you meet me after work today?"

"I'll have to. We can't possibly manage without a bed."

When I came out of the shower, Jack was on my phone.
"It's Kathy. She wants to ask you something."
"Tell her I've already gone to work."
"I'm on speaker," Kathy said.

I scowled at Jack, and mouthed, "Why didn't you say?"

"I've just been telling Jack that the kids are going to stay with Pete's parents this weekend. One of his clients gave him some vouchers for a weekend break at Rathome Manor Hotel."

"Lucky you."

"The offer is two rooms for the price of one. We thought you and Jack could come along, and we could split the remaining cost between us."

"Thanks, but we've—"

"And before you say you have plans, Jack has just told me you've got nothing on."

I mouthed to him again, "What were you thinking?"

"I know you're whispering stuff to Jack," Kathy said.

"Have you got surveillance cameras in our bedroom?"

"I don't need them. I know you."

"I've never even heard of it. Where is it?"

"North Yorkshire. So, what do you think?"

"Count us in!" Jack said before I had a chance to respond.

"Fantastic. And you haven't heard the best bit yet." Kathy hesitated—no doubt for effect. "It's haunted."

"I don't think I fancy it," I said.

"I told Pete that you'd be scared."

"I'm not scared."

"Sounds like it to me."

"Alright, we'll go, but if you're expecting to see any ghosts, you're going to be disappointed. It's obviously just a con to attract gullible people like you."

"We'll see. Bye, Jack. Bye, Sis."

"Why did you tell her we were free?" I said when Jack was off the phone.

"Because we are." He handed me my phone. "It sounds like fun."

"A haunted hotel? Do me a favour."

"It would be cool to see a ghost."

"I see them every day, and trust me, they're no more interesting than people. Anyway, the place won't really be haunted. They're probably using silly props. Actually, that's just given me an idea."

"I don't think I want to hear this." He rolled his eyes.

"If I can prove the hotel isn't really haunted, maybe we'll get our money refunded because they've been advertising under false pretences."

"If only you were joking."

***

On Mr Ivers' driveway, where his van usually stood, was a brand new car.

"What do you think of it, Jill?"

Drat. I hadn't realised that Ivers was lurking around the side of his house.

"Very nice. Is it yours?"

"It is. Not as nice as the Diamond, but more practical, I suppose."

The mention of the Diamond brought back bad memories. In a moment of insanity, I'd once agreed to go for a drive with Mr Ivers in his sports car: The Diamond. I'd never been so embarrassed as when a pushbike overtook us. It turned out that the car had the wrong engine in it. To make matters worse, Winky found a video of the sorry incident that someone had posted on YouTube. Needless to say, he has never let me forget about it since then.

"Where have you parked your van?" I said.

"I got rid of it."

"Oh? How are you going to run the movie rental business? Not from the car, surely?"

"I've closed down that business."

"Already? You only started it a couple of weeks ago. How come?"

"You were right. I should have realised that no one wants DVDs anymore. It's all about streaming."

"That must have been a difficult pill to swallow after all the start-up costs?"

"Not really. Live and learn, that's what I say."

"What are you going to do now?"

"I've already done it. Never let anyone say that Montgomery Ivers allows the grass to grow under his feet. My new business will be opening soon."

"Really? That is quick." Don't ask him what it is, Jill. Whatever you do, don't— "What kind of business is it?"

Would I never learn?

"That would be telling. All I can say is that I'm not about to make the same mistake twice. This time I've gone for something cutting-edge. Something which is guaranteed to be futureproof. I promise you'll be the first to know as soon as I'm ready to launch."

"Can't wait."

***

Lucas Morecake, the owner of the escape room, arrived at the office building at the same time as I did.

"Jill, can I introduce you to Wendy?" There was a

young witch on his arm. "My partner in life and business."

"Pleased to meet you, Wendy."

"Likewise." Her smile didn't reach her eyes, which had a darkness about them.

"Do you have a date for the opening yet?"

"It's actually this Friday. We're having a press day tomorrow. Hopefully, that will generate plenty of free publicity." He reached into his pocket. "Here's a few fifty-percent off vouchers. Feel free to use them yourself or give them to friends or relatives."

"Thanks."

"I've heard of you," Wendy said. "Aren't you *supposed* to be the most powerful witch that has ever lived?"

"Some people have said that, but I'm not sure it's possible to judge these things."

"I'm level six, you know," she said.

"That's nice for you."

"One of the youngest ever."

"Well done you."

"Come on, Wendy." Lucas started to make his way upstairs. "We've got a ton of things to do before the press day. See you around, Jill."

"Yeah. Good luck for tomorrow."

Hmm. Lucas seemed nice enough, but I'd already taken a dislike to his partner.

Mrs V was hard at work on the tapestry.

"Jill, I've just taken a call for you. I asked his name several times, but I'm still not sure I got it down correctly. I thought he said King Dollop, but it can't have been that, can it?"

"No, but it's okay. I know who it is."

"What is his name?"

"His name? It's—err—Bing."

"*Bing*?"

"Yeah. Bing—err—Gallup."

"*Bing Gallup*? It didn't sound very much like Bing Gallup."

"He does mumble a lot."

"Anyway, he wondered if you might pop over to see him later today."

"Okay, thanks. Are you feeling a little better now?"

"Yes, thank you, dear. It was just the shock of hearing about poor Patricia."

As soon as I walked into my office, Winky snapped a photo of me on his phone.

"Hey! What are you doing?"

"Relax. I'm just updating my Instagram."

"With a photo of me? I don't want my photo all over the Net."

He glanced at his phone. "You've got two likes already."

"Really? That's good, isn't it? Getting two that quickly, I mean?"

"I thought you said you didn't want your photo online?"

"I don't suppose it can do any harm. Have I got any more likes yet?"

Before he could answer, my phone rang; it was Grandma.

"Morning, Grandma."

"Whatever you have planned for this afternoon, cancel

it."

My first thought was the audacity of the woman, but then I remembered she had promised to help with my marketing, so I probably shouldn't complain.

"As it happens, I don't have too much on. What do you need me for?"

"I've decided to sell the anti-ageing cream through one of the TV shopping channels. I have an appointment there this afternoon—they're going to put together our infomercial."

"You're not going to take part in the infomercial yourself, are you?" Nobody would buy it if they thought Grandma's skin was an example of what they could expect from the cream.

"No, I've hired two models. They'll be travelling down with us."

"*Us*? Why do you need me there?"

"You'll be my assistant, of course."

"You mean your *gopher*, don't you?"

"I thought you wanted to hone your marketing skills?"

"I do, but—"

"This will be your chance to learn from an expert at first hand. Meet me outside Ever at three-thirty."

"But, Grandma, your anti-ageing cream is completely different from my business."

"Marketing is marketing. Don't be late." She hung up.

I wasn't thrilled at the prospect of being her dogsbody, but there was no denying the woman had some serious marketing chops.

"Have I got any more likes?" I asked Winky on my way out of the door.

"I thought you didn't care?"

"I don't. I'm just curious."

"I'll check." He grabbed his phone. "No."

"Still, two isn't bad, is it?"

"Hmm."

"What?"

"One of them is from someone called: IWillLikeAnyone."

"What about the other one."

"They're called: FollowMeImDesperate."

"I told you Instagram was stupid."

***

As usual, I had to shrink myself for my visit to Palace Dollop, where Chambers was on hand to meet me in the grand entrance hall.

"The king is expecting you."

"No words of advice vis-à-vis decorum this time before I go in?"

"No." He smiled. "Sorry about last time. Just our little joke."

"No problem."

"Your highness, Jill Gooder to see you."

"It's Maxwell now."

"Sorry?" Chambers looked confused.

"I recently got married. It's Jill Maxwell now."

"I beg your pardon." He turned back to the king. "Jill *Maxwell* to see you, your highness."

"Thank you, Chambers." The king walked over and shook my hand. "Nice to see you again, Jill."

"Goes it, Top Dollop?"

"On form, I see." He laughed. "Tell me about this new husband of yours."

"His name is Jack. He's a policeman."

"Is he a wizard?"

"No, he's a human, actually."

"Isn't that a little awkward?"

"Not really. We've been together for over a year now."

"And he's never suspected anything? You know—the whole witch thing?"

"No, thank goodness. My PA made it sound like your call was urgent."

"I actually called you on behalf of a good friend of mine. His name is Mr Bobb."

"A pixie, I assume?"

"Actually, no, he's a bigxie."

"A what?"

"I'm not surprised you haven't heard of them. They're related to pixies, and very similar in appearance, but with one big difference."

"What's that?"

"They're big. Hence the name: bigxie."

"What's his problem?"

"I think it might be best if Bob explains himself. With your consent, I'll have Chambers take you to see him now."

"Does he live far from here?"

"No more than ten minutes by horse and carriage. What do you say?"

"Sure. Why not?"

"Excellent. And by way of thanks, you and your husband must join me for dinner one evening."

"You're forgetting that he's a human."

"Of course. Sorry. In that case, it will be just you and me." He smirked.

Something told me that the king was quite the ladies' man.

"Slow down, Chambers!" I was holding onto the side of the carriage for dear life.

"Don't worry. I have awards for my horsemanship."

That didn't make me feel any better when the carriage went around the next bend on two wheels.

"Here we are." He pulled up the horses in front of a huge building.

"I don't suppose I need to be small any longer?" My legs felt like jelly as I climbed out of the carriage.

"No. The bigxies are human-sized."

"Are you coming in with me?"

"No, I don't want to leave the horses unattended. There's been a spate of horse thefts recently."

"I've forgotten who the king said I should ask for."

"Mr Bobb."

"Okay, thanks." I reversed the 'shrink' spell, made my way to the house, and pulled the metal chain next to the door.

A bell clanged somewhere inside, and moments later, I heard footsteps approaching.

"Can I help you?" A man peeped around the door.

"I'm here to see — err — Mr Bobb."

"Are you Jill?" He opened the door a little wider.

"Jill Maxwell, yes. King Dollop asked me to come over to see Mr Bobb."

"That's me." He opened the door. "Do come in, and please, you must call me Bob."

"Right. So, is Bob your first name or your last?"

"Both."

"Bob Bobb?"

"That's right. Let's go through to my study. Can I get you something to eat or drink?"

"No, thanks. I'm good."

"How exactly can I help?" I asked, once we were seated in the glorious oak-panelled study.

"You come highly recommended by the king. I hope you'll be as successful in solving our little problem. Can I ask, do you know much about bigxies?"

"I'll be honest. Until thirty minutes ago, I'd never heard of them."

"Don't worry. Very few people have. We've been somewhat overshadowed by our close relatives, the pixies. It's quite ironic given that we're several times larger than they are. Years ago, like many other creatures in Candlefield, the bigxies lived off the land, but then we discovered we had a particular talent that would change the whole course of our history. You're no doubt already aware that vampires don't have a reflection in a mirror?"

"Err—yeah?" I had no idea what he was talking about.

"That's where the bigxies' special talent comes into play. We provide vampires with a reflection."

"Right?" I had not the slightest idea what he was talking about.

"I can see you're puzzled. Don't worry, that's precisely the reaction we usually get. Maybe a demonstration would help?"

Chapter 4

Whenever I begin to think there can't possibly be any more levels of crazy for me to witness, I'm proven wrong.

"This is my assistant, Jim James," Bob Bobb introduced a young bigxie, who was carrying a full-length mirror.

"Pleased to meet you, Jim."

"Likewise."

"Set the mirror down over there, would you?" Bob pointed to the spot.

Only when Jim had put the mirror down did I realise it was missing one essential ingredient: glass. The 'mirror' comprised solely of the frame.

"Are you ready, Jill?" Bob said.

"I guess so. What do you want me to do?"

"Walk over to the mirror and study your reflection, please."

I laughed at what I assumed was a joke, but then I realised Bob was being serious. "But there's no glass in it?"

"Humour me, please."

"Okay." I stepped in front of the mirror, and as I did, Jim stepped behind it. And then something quite remarkable happened: Jim had transformed himself to become a mirror image of me. "Wow! That's really impressive."

"You haven't seen anything yet," Bob said. "Move around."

"Sorry?"

"Face the mirror and move around."

Feeling a touch self-conscious, I did as he said.

"Wow! That's incredible." My mirror-image (AKA Jim) was matching my movements exactly. "How does he do that?"

"It's a skill that all bigxies are born with. Of course, it wasn't a lot of use to us until one of my predecessors realised that there was a market for it."

"Vampires!"

"Precisely. Since the beginning of time, vampires have had to manage without mirrors, which as you can imagine, has resulted in some calamitous dressing faux-pas. Now, by employing a bigxie, all of that can be avoided. And, no more cutting one's chin when shaving blind." He turned to the mirror. "Thanks, Jim, that will be all."

Jim transformed back to himself, bid me goodbye, and then left us alone.

"Okay, I understand the nature of what you do now, but what exactly is it you want me to help with?"

"Someone is muscling in on our business."

"I find that hard to believe. Who else could do what Jim just did?"

"No one. At least, not to the very high standards we set ourselves. You're a witch—I assume you're familiar with the 'doppelganger' spell?"

"Yes, of course."

"Our competitor is employing witches and wizards, who are proficient at that particular spell, to work as mirror-images."

"I don't see how that could possibly work. It's one thing to be able to make yourself look like someone else, but it's an entirely different thing to be able to mirror their movements like Jim just did. I know I couldn't do it."

"Neither can they. At least not to the standards of a bigxie. The thing is, I could put up with the competition if they stuck to legitimate tactics, but they're playing dirty."

"How?"

"I have reason to believe that they've been deliberately nobbling bigxies. Every time that results in a bigxie being sacked, they step in and offer their services."

"What proof do you have of that?"

"Nothing solid as yet. That's where you come in. I'm hoping you'll be able to uncover proof of their wrongdoings, so that we can get them shut down once and for all."

"Okay, but I'm going to need a lot more information first."

"I think it would be best if you spoke to two of the bigxies who have fallen victim to this despicable sabotage. If you're willing to take on the case, I'll set up a meeting with them."

"I'm definitely up for it. Why don't you go ahead and arrange the meeting, and then give me a call when you know the where and when?"

***

Back in Washbridge, I'd arranged to meet Annette Banks' flatmate, Gaye Crooks.

"Sorry for the mess." She removed a pile of washing from one of the chairs in the living room. The place was a mess — barely one step up from a squat. "Would you like a drink?"

Having seen the state of the cups on the table, the decision was an easy one. "No, thanks. I've just had one."

"Any news on Annette?" she said.

"Not yet, but then her parents only came to see me yesterday. Have you met them?"

"A couple of times. Annette doesn't like to invite them over." She glanced around the room. "For obvious reasons."

"I don't understand why the police haven't got involved?"

"I assume that's because of the note."

"What note?"

"Didn't her parents tell you? I gave it to them the day after she took off."

"Are you saying that Annette left a note?"

"Yes. I assumed her parents would have mentioned it to you."

"They didn't. Do you know what was in it?"

"Yes, I read it, but only because it was addressed to me. It said she was feeling totally stressed out and needed to get away for a while. And that I should tell her parents that they weren't to worry."

"Right." It was beginning to look like I'd been sent on a wild goose chase. "Are you aware of any particular reason why she was feeling stressed?"

"I think it was the effort of trying to juggle work and her studies. It seemed to get much worse recently."

"Her parents told me that they gave her an allowance so that she wouldn't need to take a job."

Gaye smiled. "Annette appreciated the money they gave her, but it was barely enough to cover the rent on this dump. She took the job so she'd have money for socialising, clothes and stuff."

"What about Annette's boyfriend?"

"Her ex, you mean? Craig is okay, or at least I thought he was until he dumped her out of the blue."

"She must have been upset about that too?"

"I expected her to be, but she seemed to take it in her stride."

"I assume you haven't heard anything from Annette since the day she left the note and walked out?"

"Nothing."

"Did she take any clothes with her?"

"No."

"Doesn't that strike you as a little odd?"

"I suppose so."

"And you have no idea where she might have gone?"

"None, sorry. Do you think she's okay?"

"I don't know. Do you have a contact number for her ex-boyfriend? Craig?"

"Sure. I'll get it for you."

My meeting with Gaye had left me more than a little confused. When the Bankses came to see me, they'd failed to mention the note that their daughter had left behind. At least now, it was obvious why the police had shown no interest in Annette's disappearance. Once the Bankses had showed them the note, that would have been the end of the matter as far as they were concerned. But, why hadn't Annette's parents mentioned the note to me?

I intended to find out.

***

Oh bum! It had just turned three-twenty-five, and I was supposed to meet Grandma outside Ever at three-thirty. If

I was late, she'd kill me, so there was only one thing for it—I magicked myself to the alleyway close to the shop.

"I didn't think you were coming." Grandma tapped her watch.

"I'm on time."

"Barely."

Standing next to her were two stunningly beautiful young witches.

"Aren't you going to introduce me?" I said.

"There's no time for that." Grandma flagged down a taxi. "Get in. We don't want to be late."

Grandma sat upfront with the driver—poor man. The two witches and I sat in the back, where we made our own introductions.

"I'm Jill Gooder—err—I mean, Maxwell. I haven't got used to that yet."

"I'm Anthea," the blonde said. "Anthea Threepenny."

"And I'm Tuppence. Tuppence Lane."

"Nice to meet you both. How do you know Grandma?"

"We don't," Tuppence said. "We're from the Washtastic Model Agency. Do you know what the job is? Your grandmother hasn't really told us anything."

"She's launching a new anti-ageing cream. We're headed for the studios of one of the TV shopping channels to make an infomercial, but I can't imagine why she's hired you two for this assignment. Neither of you needs anti-ageing cream. You're both beautiful."

"Thanks," Anthea said. "Can I just say that it's an honour to meet you, Jill. I'm a big fan."

Another fan? At this rate, I'd soon have to start my own fan club.

What? Of course I was joking.

Fifteen minutes into the journey, I noticed that Tuppence had turned a shade of grey, so I asked her if she was feeling okay.

"I feel a little queasy. It might have been the sausage roll I ate. I thought it looked a strange colour."

"Will you be okay to work?"

"I think so."

After the taxi had dropped us outside the studio, I had a quiet word with Grandma.

"Tuppence isn't feeling too good. Look at her."

"She'll be alright." She turned to the two witches. "Right then, before we go inside, you both need to cast the 'ageing' spell."

Anthea and Tuppence looked confused.

"Sorry?" Anthea said.

"What's not to understand? You both know how to cast the spell, I assume?"

They nodded.

"Good. Get on with it, then."

Both women seemed uncomfortable with what she'd asked them to do, but they did it anyway. Moments later, they'd been transformed into old hags.

"What are you up to?" I said to Grandma as we made our way into the building.

Before she could respond, we were met in reception by a woman who introduced herself as Rosemary Budd who would be presenting the infomercial.

"I assume these two ladies are the models you'll be using for the shoot?"

"That's right," Grandma confirmed.

"Excellent. I'll take them through to makeup, and then come back and pick you up when we're ready to start the shoot."

"Are you doing what I think you're doing?" I said, once Grandma and I were alone.

"What are you talking about?"

"You're going to get Anthea and Tuppence to use the cream, and then reverse the 'ageing' spell, aren't you?"

"And your point is?"

"It's a deception. The cream could never have that kind of dramatic effect."

"It's called marketing, Jill. You know: the thing you've asked me to help you with."

"I'd never stoop to those depths just to promote my business."

"Which is precisely why you're on the verge of bankruptcy, and I'm building a retail empire."

Just then, Tuppence reappeared; she'd obviously reversed the 'ageing' spell.

"What are you playing at?" Grandma yelled.

"I'm sorry. I've just been sick. I can't do the shoot."

"That's great!" Grandma was as understanding as you might have expected. She turned to me. "You'll have to stand in for her."

"Me? I can't do it."

"I realise you're not as beautiful as Tuppence, but you'll just have to do."

"Sorry?"

"There's no point in apologising for your appearance. There's nothing we can do about that. Cast the 'ageing' spell and get in there sharpish."

"But, Grandma—"

"Hurry up!"

"How's Tuppence?" Anthea asked when I joined her.
"Not great."
"It was good of you to volunteer to take her place."
"Who volunteered?" I laughed.

Moments later, Rosemary Budd came to collect us for the shoot. Thankfully, she didn't seem to notice I'd swapped places with Tuppence.

When the shoot began, Grandma was centre stage. Next to her was a podium on which stood several pots of the 'wonder' cream. Rosemary Budd 'interviewed' Grandma about the exciting new product for several minutes, and then Anthea and I were wheeled on; we both looked ninety if we looked a day.

After we'd applied the product to our faces, the camera panned back to Grandma and Rosemary, who talked a little more about the cream. Finally, the camera panned back to Anthea and me, who by now had reversed the 'ageing' spell.

Rosemary's face was a picture. "Err—I have to say, that's amazing."

"Thank you, Rosemary." Grandma beamed. "And all for the bargain price of sixty-pounds a pot. A steal, I'm sure you'll agree."

As soon as the director confirmed the shoot was in the can, Grandma came over to Anthea and me.

"Go and grab a taxi before anyone asks any awkward questions."

Tuppence was waiting for us outside.

"How are you feeling?" I asked.

"Much better since I've been sick. How did the shoot go?"

"You don't want to know."

Minutes after I'd flagged down a taxi, Grandma appeared. "I think that went very well under the circumstances."

"Are you serious, Grandma? No one will be fooled into buying the cream on the strength of that infomercial."

"We'll see, shall we? The first airing is tomorrow night."

***

I wasn't able to get hold of the Bankses, so I decided to call it a day. On my drive home, I reflected on what I'd learned so far from Grandma about marketing. It could be summed up in one word: lie.

"Jill! Hello, there!" Pauline Maker called to me from across the road. "Would you like to come over for a cup of tea?"

"Thanks, but I probably should get in. I have some cleaning to catch up on."

"That's a shame. I have a delicious Victoria sponge cake."

"Go on, then. You've twisted my arm. The cleaning can wait."

"You'll have to excuse the mess." She led the way inside. "It would probably be best if we go through to the kitchen."

Mess? That didn't even begin to describe the scene of utter devastation inside the house. On our way to the kitchen, we passed by the lounge and dining room, both of which resembled small industrial units; they were full of all manner of tools and partially assembled—err—somethings.

Pauline must have seen my look of confusion, and obviously felt an explanation was called for.

"You're probably wondering what's going on in here."

"You're not installation artists, are you, by any chance? I only ask because the last people to live here were the balaclava twins."

"Who?"

"They were artists. Their most recent masterpiece was a pile of buckets."

"No, nothing like that. Shawn and I are actually inventors."

"How fascinating. Where is your husband?"

"He's in bed. He's been ill for a few days. Food poisoning, I think."

"Really? Did you know that the clowns—err—I mean, your next-door neighbours have had food poisoning? Clare and Tony, next-door to us, have been ill with it too."

"Yes, I knew about Jimmy and Kimmy, and what's more, I think I may know the source of the food poisoning."

"Oh?"

"Your other next-door neighbour, the funny little man."

"Mr Ivers?"

"That's him. He held a barbecue last Friday while you were on honeymoon. He invited everyone, but I couldn't make it because I'd promised to visit my sister. It looks like I dodged a bullet."

"I'm glad we weren't here."

Just then, my phone rang; it was Jack.

"Where are you?"

"Sorry?"

"You were meant to be meeting me at the bed shop. You've forgotten, haven't you?"

"Of course not. I've left work and I'm just getting in the car now. I'll be with you shortly."

"Another piece of sponge, Jill?" Pauline said in what she no doubt thought was a whisper.

"Who was that?" Jack said.

"Just someone on the street, giving away free samples."

"How do they know your name?"

I rubbed the phone up and down my sleeve. "The line's breaking up. I'll be with you in a few minutes."

***

Jack was waiting outside of Forty Winks.

"Sorry I'm a little late. I got delayed at the last minute."

"Eating sponge cake?"

"Very funny."

The shop, which was located on the outskirts of Washbridge, was enormous. I'd never realised there were so many different types of bed. At some point while looking around, Jack and I had become separated from one another.

"Can I help you, Madam?"

I knew that voice. When I turned around, Daze was standing behind me.

"What are you doing here?"

"Selling beds. What does it look like?"

"No, seriously, who are you after this time?"

"We're on the trail of some rogue slumber fairies."

"*Slumber* fairies? I've never heard of them."

"That's not surprising. They spend twenty-three hours a day asleep."

"What have they been up to?"

"Pickpocketing in and around Washbridge. It's been getting out of hand recently. We figured they wouldn't be far away from a bed, and where better to find one than in here?"

"Are you working solo?"

"No, it's a two-man job."

"Blaze?"

"No. He's covering the other major bed shop: Bedfordshire Beds. Laze is working with me, but I have no idea where he is. He disappeared an hour ago, the useless oaf."

"I think I've found the bed for us," Jack appeared beside me.

"You know Daze, don't you?"

"Of course. Nice to see you again."

It was all a little awkward. Daze had to pretend that she didn't know that Jack knew. Meanwhile, Jack had to pretend that he didn't know that she knew that he knew.

Try saying that quickly.

I liked the bed that Jack had picked out, so we went to the cash desk to pay for it. While we were waiting for the payment to go through, Jack nudged me.

"Look over there. There's a guy asleep in that bed."

Oh dear. Laze would be in big trouble when Daze eventually found him.

Chapter 5

As our bed was broken, Jack and I were forced to sleep on the mattress, on the floor. It didn't make much difference to me because I was totally beat, and soon drifted off into a deep sleep.

"Jill! There's someone knocking."

"Three sausages, please."

"Jill. Wake up!"

"Do you mind?" I managed to force open one eye. "I was having a fantastic dream about a full English. What time is it?"

"Just turned three."

"You must be joking!" I buried my head under the pillow. "Let me go back to my dream."

"There's someone knocking." Jack pulled the pillow off my head.

"Go and answer the door, then."

"They aren't knocking at the door. They're knocking at the bedroom window."

Right on cue, it happened again.

"See," Jack said.

"That wasn't a knock—it was more of a tap."

"Why are you arguing over semantics? There's someone at the window."

"How can there be? We're upstairs."

The tap-cum-knock came again.

We got off the mattress and walked over to the window.

"Pull back the curtain," I said.

"Why me?"

"You're the man of the house."

"Okay. On three. One, two, three."

"Joey?" I stared at the sand sloth who was gripping onto the drainpipe for dear life.

He let go with one paw to wave at us, and almost fell.

"Be careful." I opened the window. "What are you doing here?"

"Can we talk down there." He gestured towards the ground. "I don't think I can hold on much longer."

"Okay. We'll see you downstairs."

As I closed the window, Joey began to slide down the drainpipe.

"What did he say?" Jack asked.

"You heard him."

"Have you forgotten I can't understand him? All I heard was a series of squeaks."

"Oh, right." I'd forgotten Jack couldn't converse with animals. "He wants a word with us."

We both put on our dressing gowns, went downstairs and opened the back door.

"We're really sorry to bother you." Joey had his arm around Zoe's shoulder.

"You'd better come inside. It's cold out there."

The two sand sloths shared a single chair at the kitchen table.

"I'll make a cup of tea while you talk to them." Jack began to fill the kettle. "Do sand sloths drink tea?"

"I don't know." I turned to Joey. "Do you drink tea?"

"No, but a bowl of water would be nice."

"They'll just have a bowl of water."

"Okay, coming up."

"What brings you here in the middle of the night, Joey?" I said.

"We've just got back, but someone has removed our home."

"You've been gone for months. We assumed you'd moved on."

"We went to stay with my sister, Chloe, in Leeds, and we kind of lost track of the time."

"I'll say."

"Where's our sandpit gone?"

"There you go." Jack put a bowl of water on the table, and both Joey and Zoe began to lap it up feverishly.

"We had it removed," I said. "We thought you'd gone for good."

Joey wiped his lips. "Where will we live now?"

"There must be other sandpits around here."

"Will you help us to find one? It's really dangerous for us after dark. There are so many predators lurking."

"What's he saying?" Jack joined us at the table.

"He wants us to help them to find another sandpit."

"Now?"

"It's either that or let them stay in the house tonight."

Jack whispered in my ear, "They smell."

He was right. Cute as they were, the sand sloths gave off a rather unpleasant odour.

"Okay. We'll help you, but we'll need to get changed first."

Jack and I left the two little creatures in the kitchen while we went upstairs to get dressed.

"How are we supposed to find a sandpit?" Jack said.

"I don't know. Drive around until we spot one, I suppose."

"We'll never see one from the road. They're always in the back gardens."

"We'll think of something."

Once we were dressed, Joey and Zoe followed us out of the house.

"We'll take your car," I said.

"No chance." Jack blocked my way. "I don't want that smell in my car."

"It's a good job they don't know what you're saying. Okay, we'll take mine."

I drove to the next village because I figured that we were less likely to be recognised there.

"Go on, then," I said, after pulling up in a cul-de-sac on a new housing estate.

"Me?" Jack looked horrified. "Why me?"

"You were the one who wanted me to drive, and besides, if anyone sees you, you can flash your warrant card, and tell them you're looking for burglars."

"Dressed like this?" He was wearing one of his bowling shirts and a pair of shorts.

"Tell them you're undercover."

He climbed out of the car, and then started at one end of the street, and worked his way down. I was beginning to think we were out of luck when he emerged from behind the last house, but then he gave me the thumbs up.

"Okay. This is your new home." I jumped out of the car and let Joey and Zoe out of the back. "Good luck, you two."

"Thanks, Jill." Joey took Zoe's hand, and they disappeared down the driveway.

"Sometimes, I think I preferred it when I didn't know you were a witch," Jack said when he got back into the car. "Life was so much simpler then."

"For you, maybe."

***

When I got up the next morning, I felt sleep-deprived. Jack didn't look much better.

"You and your brilliant ideas," he said.

"What are you talking about?"

"You were the one who suggested getting rid of the sandpit."

"How was I supposed to know that Joey and Zoe would be back? And besides, I don't want them living in our back garden."

"I just hope no one saw me last night or I'll have some explaining to do."

"Just tell them you were helping to rehome a couple of sand sloths."

"You're hilarious. Oh, by the way, I meant to mention that I took a look at the hit-and-run you asked about. There's nothing to suggest it was deliberate. They found the car burnt out a few miles away. Looks like joy-riders."

"Why do they call it that?"

"Don't ask me. There's rarely much joy involved."

"Thanks for checking, anyway."

"I'd like you to do me a favour in return."

"Do we have time?"

"Not that kind of favour. I should have paid the final bill for the reception yesterday, but I forgot all about it. Can you drop by there today and pay it?"

"Why me?"

"Because I'm going to be in West Chipping all day, and it's on your way into work."

"Okay, I suppose so."

"You should try to get them to give you a bit of a discount while you're at it."

"Why would they do that?"

"To compensate for the smell of cat. I noticed it during the ceremony and at the reception. A few other people mentioned it too. I reckon they must have left a cat indoors overnight."

"Actually, that's not what happened."

"It must have —. Hold on, you know something about it, don't you?"

"I might do."

"Come on. What do you know?"

"You remember when Mikey dropped out from being a pageboy?"

"Yeah?"

"Well, I'd kind of promised Winky that if that happened, he could take his place."

"Have a cat as a pageboy?"

"Pagecat."

"There's no such thing."

"I only promised him because I didn't think there was any chance it would happen. But then, when it did, I didn't know how to let him down. I did try to send him to the wrong hotel, but he realised and found us anyway. He did look very smart, though."

"How come I didn't see him there?"

"I couldn't let anyone see him because they would have thought I was crazy."

"You think?"

"I made him invisible."

"Are you telling me that your invisible cat was at the

ceremony and reception?"

"When you say it like that, it sounds kind of weird, but yes, he walked behind Kathy and Lizzie down the aisle."

"You couldn't make this stuff up."

***

Jack had already left by the time I set out for work.

"Morning, Jill!" Mr Ivers shouted.

"Morning, Mr Ivers."

"You really must start to call me Monty."

"Right." Just then, I remembered what Pauline Maker had told me. "Have you been feeling okay, Mr—err—Monty?"

"Never better. Firing on all cylinders."

"I was talking to Pauline from across the road. Her husband has been laid up with food poisoning. One or two of the other neighbours have gone down with it too."

"How terrible—I had no idea."

"Pauline mentioned that they'd all been to a barbecue at your place."

"I can't believe it could be anything they ate at the barbecue or I would have been ill too. I'm always very careful when it comes to grilling meat."

"Is there anything the others ate that you didn't?"

"Nothing. Oh, there was one thing." He started for the door. "Wait there a minute." Moments later, he reappeared with a bowl of berries. "I don't normally buy fruit because it brings me out in a rash, but these were on offer, so I got them for my guests. They seemed to go down very well."

"I don't think I've seen those before. What kind are

they?"

"Candleberries, apparently."

"I can't say I've ever heard of them."

"Me neither. I really don't think it could have been these that made the others ill." He offered the bowl. "Would you like to try some?"

"I don't think I should."

"Fair enough."

"They do look nice, though. Maybe just a couple." I grabbed a handful.

What? Come on, you should know the *couple* rule by now.

"They're delicious."

"You can have the rest if you'd like them. I won't be eating them."

"Okay, thanks. I'll take them inside — Jack and I can have them after dinner tonight."

"I'd better get going, Jill. There's lots of work still to do on my new business venture."

"Still not ready to tell me what it is?"

"Sorry, but if I told you, I'd be forced to kill you."

***

I'd managed to get hold of the Bankses, and they'd agreed to meet with me at their house. Fortunately, they lived close to Washbridge Park Hotel, so I was able to nip in there first to pay the bill (no cat-odour reductions were requested).

The Bankses had a delightful detached house located on a quiet tree-lined road. For reasons known only to them, they'd chosen to paint the front of the house in a sickly strawberry colour.

Christine Banks answered the door and led me through to the conservatory where her husband was doing the Times crossword. After serving tea and biscuits, Christine joined us.

"I went to see Annette's flatmate, Gaye, yesterday." I took a bite of shortbread (a poor substitute for custard creams, but I was feeling peckish).

"Lovely girl." Christine obviously approved.

"She told me something that I found a little disconcerting."

"Does she know something about Annette?" Gordon said.

"No. She told me that Annette had left a note, which she'd passed to you."

"Oh that."

"Why didn't you tell me about it?"

"We thought if we did that you'd refuse to take the case. As soon as the police found out about it, they lost all interest."

"Do you have the note?"

"I'll fetch it." Christine disappeared out of the room, and moments later, returned with it in her hand.

The note was brief and to the point. "I'll be honest with you. This seems to make it pretty clear that she wanted to get away because she was feeling stressed."

"What could she possibly have been stressed about?" Gordon said.

"You're going to find out sooner or later, so I may as well tell you now. Annette had been holding down a part-time job as well as going to college."

"She never said anything about a job to us." Christine looked genuinely surprised.

"She didn't think you'd approve."

"Why would she take a job?" Gordon said. "We give her an allowance."

"She appreciated the help you give her, but it wasn't enough to cover all of her expenses. It's clear to me that she needs a little time away from the stresses of work and college. I'm sure she'll come back when she's had the chance to clear her head."

"It's not like Annette," Gordon said. "I just don't buy it."

"Are you saying the note wasn't written by your daughter?"

"No, that's definitely Annette's handwriting, but I still think there's more to it. I'd like you to stay on the case."

"But you'll be wasting your money."

"It's ours to waste."

"Fair enough, but you must understand that I can't force your daughter to come home against her will."

"Of course not, but if you could at least find her, and confirm that she's alright, that would give us peace of mind."

"Okay, I'll stick with it for now."

***

I'd skipped breakfast, so by the time I got into town, I was starving. For some unknown reason, I had a craving for a burger and fries, so I called in at Burger Bay.

When I saw the length of the queues, I almost changed my mind, but my stomach insisted I stay. I would have used one of the self-order machines, but they all had 'out of order' notices stuck to them.

When I eventually made it to the front of the queue, the spotty young man behind the counter looked as though he would have chosen to be anywhere but there.

"Can I get a cheeseburger, fries and a diet coke, please?"

"That will be four pounds-twenty, please."

I handed him the cash. "What's wrong with the self-order machines?"

"They've never been right since they installed them. The old ones were much better."

"What's wrong with them?"

"We keep getting 'ghost' orders coming through."

"How do you mean: 'ghost' orders?"

"Orders that no one has placed. Sometimes, even when we have no customers in the shop, an order will come through. It got to the point where we didn't know which orders were real and which weren't. The supplier's been trying to sort them out for ages, but I don't think they have a clue what's wrong with them."

"Right, thanks." I took my food, grabbed a table in sight of the counter, and made a call.

"Pearl, it's Jill."

"Hi, Jill."

"Can you do something for me?"

"Sure. What is it?"

"Can you go on one of the self-order machines and place an order for nuggets, fries and a chocolate milkshake?"

"Why?"

"Humour me, please."

"Okay. I'll just put the phone down."

I watched the counter, and sure enough, moments later, I saw the terminal spring into life. The spotty young man noticed it too and shook his head.

"Excuse me!" I shouted to him. "Is that another 'ghost' order?"

"Yeah."

"Can you tell me what it's for?"

He obviously thought I was a nutter, but ripped off the slip and handed it to me. "It's no good to us, anyway."

"Thanks."

"Jill!" Pearl was back on the phone. "I've done it. Do you want to tell me what this is all about?"

"All in good time. Thanks, Pearl. Bye."

While I ate my meal, I kept a lookout for one of the managers.

"Excuse me."

"Yes, Madam. How can I help?"

"Do you happen to have the contact details for the people who supplied your self-order machines?"

"If you're thinking of buying some, I wouldn't bother. They're next to useless."

"Still, I'd like the contact details if you have them."

"Okay. Wait there while I dig them out."

Chapter 6

When I arrived at the office, I was momentarily puzzled by the amount of activity down the corridor, but then I remembered that it was Escape's press day.

"I wish you'd told me that you were expecting a large parcel, Jill," Mrs V looked somewhat disgruntled.

"I'm not."

"Well, one arrived thirty minutes ago, and it took two men to carry it up the stairs. They were absolutely exhausted, so I made them a cup of tea and gave them a scarf each."

"That was very kind of you. I'd better go and see what it is."

Winky was busy tearing open the large box.

"Do you mind?" I tried to shoo him away. "I didn't say you could open my parcels."

"This is mine. Look, it's addressed to me."

The label read:

Mr W. Inky

c/o Gooder & Maxwell.

"What's with the *Gooder & Maxwell*?"

"That's what the sign says, isn't it? Stand back and let me finish unpacking it."

When he'd taken the machine out of the box, I was none the wiser. "What is it?"

"It's a state-of-the-art digital knitting machine."

"And you want that for—?"

"Seeing as how the old bag lady has refused to include me in her tapestry, I'm going to produce one of my own."

"This should be good." I laughed.

"It won't be good, it will be amazing. Have you seen her tapestry? It's rubbish. It's just lots of little blocks of colour which are supposed to look like you and her. Pah!"

"How do *you* know what it looks like?"

"I'm all seeing. You should know that by now. Anyway, my tapestry will be produced from digitised images of actual photographs."

"So that's why you wanted a photo of me yesterday?"

"Yes, but I did put it on Instagram as well."

"Have I got any more likes, by the way."

"I'll check." He took out his phone. "Oh dear."

"What?"

"FollowMeImDesperate has cancelled his like. Presumably he changed his mind because you didn't follow him back."

"As if I care. What's this lot going to cost you?"

"Not much. I've got the machine on one-week's free trial. I'll return it before the week is out."

"That's dishonest."

"I prefer to think of it as tactical smarts."

"The wool will still cost you a pretty penny. You can't get that on a free trial."

"I don't need to. I'll use the Everlasting Wool subscription."

"Since when did you have a subscription to Everlasting Wool?"

"I don't, but the old bag lady does, and I know her log-in details."

"Do you have no scruples?"

"Nah, I sold them on eBay."

"That machine looks very complicated. Are you sure

you'll be able to work it?"

"Course. Piece of cake."

Winky's expression suddenly changed, and he scurried under the sofa. I was just about to ask him what was wrong when I noticed the temperature had dropped.

"Morning, Jill." The colonel appeared with Priscilla on his arm.

"Morning, you two. I haven't seen you for a while."

"I hear you've gone and got yourself married in the meantime."

"I have indeed. I'm now Jill Maxwell."

"Congratulations, Jill." Priscilla beamed. "I couldn't be happier for you."

"Is Jack going to come and work with you in the business?" the colonel said.

"No. If we worked together, we'd probably end up killing one another. What made you ask that?"

"Your new sign?"

"Oh, that stupid thing. No, that's a mistake. It should read Jill Maxwell. Hopefully, it will be replaced soon."

"We won't take up much of your time. I just wanted to drop by to let you know that I'm standing for election to COG."

"What's that?"

"The Council Of Ghosts. I suppose you could call it a kind of city council for Ghost Town. The elections are in a couple of weeks."

"Good for you. I hope it has more clout than the Combined Sup Council. I was elected to that some time ago, but I resigned once I realised it was just a talking shop that actually achieved nothing."

"Here you are, Jill." Priscilla handed me a rosette with a

photo of the colonel on it.

"I trust I can count on your vote," he said.

"I don't actually think I qualify to vote."

He laughed. "Silly me. What was I thinking? But maybe you'll lend me your support by wearing the rosette when you're in GT?"

"Of course. I'll be happy to."

As soon as the colonel and Priscilla had left, Winky reappeared.

"You shouldn't allow those ghosts to drop in here like that."

"You're not afraid of them, are you?"

"Of course not." He scoffed, somewhat unconvincingly. "They just make the room cold."

***

"I have a couple of visits to make, Mrs V. I probably won't get back into the office today."

"Okay, dear. I'll see you in the morning. By the way, what was in the parcel?"

"Err—it was nothing. It must have been sent to me by mistake. I'm going to have it collected."

Just then, two men came into the outer office: One was carrying a camera, the other had one of those furry microphone things.

What? How am I supposed to know the correct terminology? Sheesh!

"Can I help you?" I said.

"Alright, love. Is this the escape thingy?" The articulate young man with the microphone took a puff on his electronic cigarette.

"No, it isn't, and I'd rather you didn't smoke that thing in here."

"Keep your wig on." He took a piece of paper out of his pocket. "This is the address I've got. Are you sure this isn't the right gaff?"

There were times when I simply despaired.

"You're looking for Escape. Go back out of the door you just came in and along the corridor."

"Oh, right. Thanks. What is it you do, then?"

"I'm a private investigator."

"That's funny." He laughed. "No, seriously, what is it you really do?"

"I *really* am a private investigator."

"But you're a woman?"

"Well spotted. Now, if you wouldn't mind, we're rather busy."

"You can investigate me anytime, sweetheart," he said, on his way out of the door.

If Mrs V and the man's sidekick hadn't been there, I would have taken great pleasure in turning him into the rat he quite obviously was.

***

The manager of Burger Bay had given me the address for Ron Gunn, the man who had supplied them with the new self-order machines. I didn't ring in advance of my visit because I had a sneaking suspicion he'd be in no hurry to see me. Instead, I just turned up at his factory—a small industrial unit on the Washtide Estate.

"Good afternoon." The bubbly young witch on

reception had a sparkly blue ribbon in her hair.

"Hi. I'd like to see Ron Gunn, please."

"Do you have an appointment?"

"No, but I'd like to see him anyway."

"He doesn't usually see people without an appointment."

"Tell him that he's entitled to a development grant, but I'll need him to complete the paperwork today."

"A what?"

"Development grant."

"Right." She picked up the phone and pressed a single key. "Dad, there's a woman here who says you're entitled to a—" She looked to me for help.

"Development grant."

"A development ant."

"Grant."

"Grant." She giggled. "Not an ant. That would just be silly." She put down the phone. "He says he can spare you five minutes."

"Thank you. I take it this is a family business?"

"Yeah. Ron's my dad. I'm Ann."

Ron's office, which was on the shop-floor of the unit, smelled of coffee and grease.

"Ann said something about a grant?" He glanced up from the small circuit board he was working on.

"Yeah, actually, I lied about that."

That seemed to get his attention. "Who are you, then? What do you want?"

"I'd like you to remove the self-order machines you installed in Cuppy C, and refund the money to the twins."

"Dream on." He laughed. "They got exactly what they

paid for."

"No, they didn't. They paid for machines which should have been reconfigured to match their menu. All you did was change the pictures on the screen. You conned them."

"I think you'd better leave."

"If I do, I'll go straight to Burger Bay, and tell them why their machines aren't working."

"Like they'll listen to you." He scoffed.

"I think they will. Especially when I'm able to produce 'ghost' orders at will."

"What do you know about 'ghost' orders?"

"You haven't worked it out yet, have you? The 'ghost' orders at Burger Bay are coming from the machines you offloaded to Cuppy C."

"Okay, I'll reconfigure the Cuppy C machines."

"It's too late for that. The twins don't want them now. You have to take them out and refund all their money."

"I can't afford to do that."

"I'm confident you'll find a way. I'd wager that Burger Bay is one of your largest customers. They've probably ordered machines for all of their outlets. Am I right?" He didn't answer, but then he didn't need to because the look on his face confirmed my suspicions. "They probably paid you to dispose of the old machines, didn't they? If they find out that you've been selling them on, they won't be very pleased."

"Okay, okay. I'll take the machines out of Cuppy C."

"And refund all of their money?"

"Yes, yes, alright. I'll do it tomorrow."

"Today or I go to Burger Bay."

"Okay, today."

After leaving Ron Gunn, I magicked myself over to Cuppy C.

"I have good news for you, Pearl."

"I could do with some. Just look at this place." Cuppy C was empty except for an elderly couple who were sitting by the window. "It's been like this all day."

"Any idea why?"

"Haven't you heard about the flu?"

"No."

"There's been an outbreak of sup flu. It's the first one for over twenty years. I was just a kid when the last one struck."

"Are Lily and Lil okay?"

"Yeah, it doesn't seem to affect kids, fortunately."

"What about Amber and Aunt Lucy?"

"We're all okay up to now, touch wood, but it's extremely contagious, so it's probably only a matter of time until we all go down with it. Luckily, it usually only lasts for a few days. Anyway, you said you had some good news for me?"

"You'll be pleased to hear that Ron Gunn will be coming around later to remove these useless machines, and to give you a full refund."

"How did you manage that?" She looked well and truly gobsmacked.

"I just appealed to his better nature."

"I know that's not true, but however you managed it, thanks. That money will come in handy."

Just then, I spotted an unfamiliar face behind the counter in the cake shop.

"Is she a new recruit?"

"Yeah, Carol left last week to go and work in the human

world. Gloria started on Monday."

"Is she settling in alright?"

"It's hard to tell because it's been so quiet in here there's been nothing to test her. Did you want a drink or something to eat?"

"Err—no, I won't bother. I thought I'd pop over to see Aunt Lucy."

"Okay. Thanks again for sorting out the machines."

***

Aunt Lucy spotted me coming up the driveway. When she met me at the door, she had a feather duster in her hand.

"Where's Lily?"

"I've just put her down, so I thought I'd catch up on a bit of housework while she's asleep."

"I'd better leave you to it, then."

"Don't be silly. The dust will still be there later. Come on through to the kitchen and I'll make us both a nice cup of tea."

"Pearl was just telling me about the sup flu."

"Quite a few of my friends are laid up with it. I'm keeping my fingers crossed we can avoid it."

"Where's Barry?"

"Dolly has taken him for the day. He'll be exhausted when he gets back—he always is. To be honest, I wish she'd take the tortoise too."

"Rhymes? He can't be causing you any problems, surely?"

"Not really." She smiled. "It's just that poetry of his. He's relentless, and they're all terrible."

"I hope you haven't said that to him?"

"Of course not. That's the problem. I made the mistake of praising his first poem, and since then, he's written one for me every day." She pointed to a pile of paper. "Look at all those."

"Oh dear."

"Just listen to this one:
Jill calls her Aunt, but I call her Lucy,
Her eyes are beautiful, just like the blue sea,
She bakes cakes galore, the oven's always hot,
And when Jill comes around, she eats the lot."

"I see what you mean. That is pretty awful."

"Accurate, though." She grinned.

Cheek!

After we'd finished our tea and biscuits (and before you ask, I only had a couple), I was about to leave, but Aunt Lucy said there was something she wanted to show me in the garden.

"Come and look what we found in the far corner. It was Lester who noticed them first." She pointed to a bush, which had berries identical to those that Mr Ivers had given to me.

"Candleberries."

"You've seen them before, then?"

"Yeah, one of our neighbours gave me some this morning."

"How on earth did he get hold of them?"

"From the corner shop, apparently."

"I hope he didn't eat any."

"It's okay. They're very nice. I had a handful this

morning."

"They're okay for you, but not for humans. If a human eats these berries, they'll get food poisoning, and it can be quite nasty."

"Oh no! Oh, no, no, no!"

"What's wrong, Jill?"

"I put a bowlful of them in the fridge. If Jack—"

"You'd better get back there now."

I didn't need telling twice. There was no time to stop off in Washbridge to pick up my car. Instead, I magicked myself straight back to the house. When I landed in the hall, I could hear sounds coming from the kitchen.

Oh no!

"These look nice." Jack had the bowl in his hand. "What kind of berry are they?"

He was just about to pick one up when I hurled myself across the kitchen and knocked the bowl from his hand. It smashed into a dozen pieces and spilled the berries all over the kitchen floor.

"What was that all about?" Jack looked at me like I'd lost my mind. "If you wanted them all for yourself, you only had to say."

"They're poisonous." Without thinking, I picked one up and ate it.

"It looks like it."

"No, honestly, they are. These are Candleberries from Candlefield. They're okay for sups but poisonous to humans. That's why all of our neighbours have been ill."

"Where did they come from?"

"Mr Ivers told me he got them from the corner shop. I'm going to go down there now to make sure they don't sell any more."

***

Lucy Locket was behind the counter.

"Hi, Lucy. Is Jack in?"

"He's here somewhere."

"Any chance of getting him for me? I could do with a quick word."

"Sure." She took a walkie-talkie out of her pocket. "Corner One to Corner Two. Come in."

"Corner Two receiving, over."

"Jill would like to speak with you."

"On my way. Corner Two out."

Moments later, Little Jack Corner appeared. He seemed so much smaller when he wasn't standing on his box.

"What can I do for you, Jill?"

"My next-door neighbour tells me that he bought some Candleberries from you."

"He did, but I'm afraid you're out of luck. I only bought a small batch, and your neighbour took them all."

"Thank goodness for that. They're poisonous."

"Are you sure?"

"Positive. A number of people on my street have had bad bouts of food poisoning."

"I'm so sorry. I had no idea."

"It's not your fault, Jack—you weren't to know. Can you tell me who you got them from?"

"I'm afraid I don't know anything about him. It was a cash transaction and he didn't leave any contact details."

"That's a shame. Would you let me know if he comes around again?"

"Of course."

***

While Jack made dinner, I magicked myself back to Washbridge to pick up the car. By the time I'd driven home, dinner was served. Very delicious it was too.

After we'd finished, I put the remaining berries in a bowl, and covered them in cream.

"You're surely not going to eat those?" Jack said.

"Why not? You know the five-second rule."

"I don't mean that. Do you think it's fair to eat them in front of me when I can't have any?"

"You're right. It was very thoughtless of me. Why don't you go through to the lounge? That way, you won't see me eating them."

"You're unbelievable. You can do the washing up, then."

After I'd finished eating the delicious berries, and loaded the dishwasher, I went to join Jack in the lounge where he was glued to the TV.

"What's that you're watching?"

"A documentary. It's quite interesting, actually. That guy, Mark Sobers, is only thirty-five, but he's already made several million from a network of care homes."

"Riveting." I yawned. "Can I change stations for a minute?"

"Hold on." He was too late. I'd already flipped channels. "Isn't that your grandmother?"

"Yeah, it's her infomercial for the anti-ageing cream she's peddling now."

"That old girl on the left looks familiar. Where do I

know her from?"

"No idea. I've never seen her before in my life." I quickly switched the channel back. "Sorry, I didn't mean to interrupt your viewing."

Chapter 7

The next morning, Jack was back in front of the television—this time to catch up on TenPin TV.

"Don't you ever get bored with bowling?" I managed in-between yawns.

"That's like saying: do you get bored of life. Hey, you never told me about the escape room that's opening next door to your offices."

"Nothing much to tell. How do you know about it, anyway?"

"There was an item on the local news earlier. It looks great—we should definitely check it out sometime."

"I don't really see the point in escape rooms."

"There doesn't have to be a *point* to everything. They're just fun."

"If you say so. The owners are sups, and I'm a bit concerned they're going to use magic to power their enterprise. If they do, and it gets out, the publicity could affect me."

"Why would it affect you?"

"If the press gets wind of some kind of supernatural story, they'll come buzzing around the building, asking questions."

"I'm sure you can handle the press. Anyway, I'd still like to give it a try some time. We could ask Kathy and Peter if they're up for it."

"That reminds me, what time are we supposed to be meeting them on Saturday?"

"Ten o'clock. I said we'd take my car."

"Did you now? So, you don't mind using your car to ferry my sister and her husband around, but you wouldn't use it when we were helping the sand sloths to find a sandpit."

"Kathy and Peter don't smell."

"You obviously haven't been around Kathy after one of her yoga sessions."

As soon as Jack's programme had ended, I grabbed the remote control. "I want to watch — err — the news."

"Since when did you watch the morning news?"

"I often do. You know I like to keep abreast of current affairs."

When he'd left the room, I switched to the shopping channel. I didn't have to wait long before Grandma's infomercial aired. Seeing the aged version of myself wasn't a pleasant experience, so I focussed on the sales ticker at the bottom of the screen. The number of units sold was already into four figures. At sixty-pounds a pop, Grandma had to be coining it, but I couldn't help but wonder what would happen once the customers had tried the cream, and realised that it couldn't perform the miracles shown in the advert.

***

When I arrived at the office building, Mrs V was waiting for me at the top of the stairs.

"Have you forgotten your key, Mrs V?"

"I never forget it. You should know that."

"Sorry, I just thought — "

"I can't get through the door."

"Here, let me try." I pushed it, but it wouldn't budge. It felt as though something was wedged behind it.

Just then, who should come strolling up the stairs but Winky.

"What are you waiting for?" He scratched at the door. "I'm starving."

"It won't open."

"I know that," Mrs V said. "I just told you."

"Sorry, I was thinking out loud. Do you think you could go and get us a coffee while I try to figure out what's wrong here?"

"I don't drink coffee."

"Of course." I handed her a ten-pound note. "Get yourself a cup of tea."

"I don't hold with paying the exorbitant amounts they charge in those coffee shops."

"I know, but needs must on this occasion."

As soon as Mrs V was out of earshot, I turned to Winky. "Do you know anything about this?"

"Why would I? I spent the night at Digger's."

"Who's he?"

"An old buddy of mine who I haven't seen for ages."

"Is he Australian?"

"Nah. When we were young, he was always going around saying, *I dig this,* and *I dig that.* Hence the name."

"Are you sure everything was okay when you left the office last night?"

"Yeah, I set the knitting machine going, and then—" His expression suddenly changed to one of horror.

"What?"

"Nothing."

"Winky! Tell me!"

"I'm just trying to remember if I set the max length for the tapestry." He laughed, nervously. "I'm sure I did."

"What would happen if you didn't?"

"It would just keep going until the wool ran out."

"Everlasting Wool never runs out."

"Whoops."

"Are you telling me that the reason I can't get through the door is because the office is full of your tapestry?"

"It's possible, I guess."

"And presumably, the knitting machine is still hard at work? What happens when there's no more room in there?"

"I'm sure that won't happen."

"I'm not. If there's nowhere else for it to go, it's probably going to burst through the windows." I nudged him with my foot. "Stand aside."

"What are you going to do?"

"Be quiet! Let me think."

Eventually, with the help of the 'power' spell, I was able to push the door open a matter of centimetres. That was enough to confirm my suspicions. The room was filled from floor to ceiling with tapestry.

The 'shrink' spell took every ounce of my strength, but eventually it did the trick, and I managed to miniaturise the tapestry, which allowed the door to open.

"How did you manage to get in?" Mrs V returned right on cue.

"I—err—the door just popped open. The wood must have warped a little."

Once we were inside, Winky grabbed the tiny tapestry and bolted for my office.

"Where did all these bits of wool come from?" Mrs V ran her hand over her desk. "If that cat has been in my wool basket again, I'll murder him."

When I went through to my office, Winky was nowhere to be seen.

"Get out here!"

"I'm asleep." The voice came from under the sofa.

"Now!"

He crept out. "I suppose you're going to blame me for this?"

"Who else am I supposed to blame? I want that machine sent back today."

"But I haven't finished my tapestry yet."

"Today, and you can sweep up all these bits of wool too."

"But I've been up all night. I'm beat."

"Do I look like I care?"

"You've really changed since you got married."

***

Winky was still sweeping the office (and moaning) when my phone rang.

"Jill? It's Bob Bobb."

"Hi, Bob."

"I've managed to get hold of the two bigxies I mentioned, and they're both happy to talk to you. Is there any chance you could meet with them this afternoon?"

"I don't see why not. Where did you have in mind?"

"There's a coffee shop here in Candlefield called Slurp. It's just off the main market square. How does two o'clock sound?"

"Sounds good. What are their names?"

"Johnny Johnson and Mickey Michaels."

"Okay. Tell them I'll see them later."

"Thanks, Jill."

"Can I stop sweeping now?" Winky said.

"You haven't done that corner yet."

"What did your last slave die of?"

At that moment, the door opened, and Mrs V stepped into my office. Fortunately, Winky had the foresight to drop the brush before she saw him with it.

"Jill, that horrible man, Mr Bugle, is out there. He's with another man. Shall I tell him to get lost?"

"No, it's okay. Show them in, would you?"

"Are you sure?"

"Yeah, I think I know what it's about. It'll be okay."

"I'm not making him a drink."

"That's alright. I doubt he'll be here for long."

"Good, and he needn't think I'm going to give him a scarf either."

"Fair enough."

The man with Dougal Andrews looked pale and drawn.

"Jill, this is Frank Lewis. Donna Lewis' husband."

"I'm sorry for your loss, Mr Lewis."

"Thank you." He sounded dazed.

"Why don't you both have a seat?"

Dougal had to practically guide his friend onto one of the chairs.

"Jill, did you ask your husband about the hit-and-run?" Dougal said.

"Yes. He said there was nothing to suggest it had been deliberate. The car was found burnt out a few miles from the incident. It looks like so-called joy riders."

Dougal shook his head. "He's wrong."

"Someone murdered her," Frank looked me in the eye. "She was afraid something like this was going to happen." He pulled himself up in the chair. "Donna has worked undercover for as long as I've known her, and she's got herself into a few dodgy situations before, but this time was different. She was really scared."

"What did she tell you about the story she was working on?"

"Nothing, but then she never did. She wouldn't talk about the stories until they were in the bag and published."

"I suggested Frank should come here today," Dougal said. "I know you and I don't always see eye to eye, and I realise that I've sometimes crossed the line." That was probably the understatement of the year. "But I've come to respect the work you do. The truth is, you probably solve more crimes in Washbridge than the police do. Donna was a dear friend, and if anyone can find out what happened to her, it's probably you."

I was stunned, and before I could respond, Frank said, "I can pay you."

"It's not going to be easy if no one knows what she was working on."

"I'd still like you to try," Frank said. "Please."

"Okay. You'd better tell me everything you can about Donna."

After Dougal and Frank had left, Winky came out from under the sofa. "How about some food? I'm starving."

"What's the magic word?"

"Salmon?"

"Try: *please*."

"Please can I have some food before I expire? I'm worn out with all the sweeping."

"You haven't finished yet. Do that corner, and then I'll give you something to eat."

He moaned and groaned but did as I asked. When he'd finished, I gave him a bowl of food.

"This isn't salmon."

"It's all I've got until I go to the shops."

"This place is going to the dogs."

***

I'd promised to meet my mother in Spooky Wooky. When she'd rung, she'd said there was something she wanted to talk to me about, but when I'd asked what it was, she'd been very cagey, so I was intrigued to discover what she had on her mind. And, hopefully, I'd be able to get a decent cup of coffee instead of that awful dishwater that Mrs V had bought.

"Long time no see, Jill." Larry greeted me with a smile. "I hear you've gone and got yourself married."

"That's right. I'm young, free and single no longer."

"Blueberry muffin?" Harry appeared at Larry's side.

"Not today. I'm trying to cut down on them."

"You're hilarious." He laughed.

"No, honestly, I really am. I'll just have a caramel latte. I'm supposed to be meeting my mother here. I take it she hasn't been in yet?"

"Not yet." Harry went over to the back counter to make my drink.

"I assume you've heard about the upcoming elections?"

Larry said.

"For COG?"

"Yes. Harry is standing for election, and I'm acting as his campaign manager. I trust we can rely on your support?"

"Err, actually—" I pulled out the colonel's rosette from my pocket.

"Looks like she's on the other team, Harry."

Harry gave me a disappointed look.

"I'm sorry, guys. I had no idea you were standing, and I've known the colonel for ages."

"It's okay, Jill," Harry said. "The colonel is a good man. It's just a pity he's going to lose."

"Jill, sorry I'm late." My mother appeared, red-faced and out of breath. "I was cleaning Alberto's gnomes, and I lost all track of time."

"No problem. I've only just got here myself."

We made the usual small talk for five minutes or so, but then curiosity got the better of me.

"You said there was something you wanted to talk to me about?"

"That's right. You'll be pleased to know that your father and I are getting along much better now. Alberto and Blodwyn too. The four of us meet up at least a couple of times each week."

"That's great. All the squabbling was getting rather tiresome."

"I'm sorry you had to put up with that nonsense. Anyway, the other night, we were all at your father's house, and we got talking about the human world."

"Oh?"

"Don't get me wrong, we all like GT. Alberto and I

couldn't be happier in our little house. But the thing is, we'd all like to spend more time in the human world — we all kind of miss it."

"Well, you know you're welcome to pay me a visit from time to time."

"We know that, but we were thinking of a more permanent arrangement."

"How do you mean: *permanent*?"

"A base we can call our own. Somewhere we can visit whenever we want, for as long as we want."

"I see. A sort of haunting."

"That's such an ugly word." She pulled a face. "I'd like to think of it more as a kind of holiday home."

"Right. Did you have anywhere in mind?"

"Yes, we thought we could use your house."

"My house?" I almost spat out the coffee.

"It's the obvious place."

"Sorry, but that's not happening."

"Jack wouldn't mind, I'm sure."

"*I* would, though. I don't want to share our house with my parents. No offence."

"We thought you'd jump at the chance."

"You were very much mistaken, then. You'll have to have a rethink."

"I don't suppose you know of anyone who would appreciate having four ghosts for company?"

"Weirdly enough, no."

"Oh well." She sighed. "We were so looking forward to spending more time in the human world, but if it's not to be —"

"Look, I'll give it some thought and see if I can come up with any bright ideas."

"Would you, Jill?" She stood up, walked around the table, and gave me a hug. "We'd be so very grateful."

"Just don't go getting your hopes up."

After we'd finished our drinks, my mother had to shoot off to buy fish for Alberto's dinner. I was just about to leave too when Constance Bowler walked in. Boy, did she look harassed.

"Are you okay, Constance?"

"Not really. We've got a bit of a situation. I haven't had anything to eat yet today, so I thought I'd just grab a scone and a drink."

"What's happened? Can you talk about it?"

"Between you and me, there's been a breakout from GT maximum security prison. Oswald Mean, a real nasty piece of work, is on the loose. He's got a string of convictions and is very dangerous."

"Is there anything I can do to help?"

"Thanks, but I don't think so. We've got all available officers working on it, and there's an appeal going out on the radio and TV later. Hopefully, someone will spot him, and we'll be able to catch him before he can hurt anyone." She took out her phone and pulled up a photo. "That's him."

"He looks like a thug."

"He is. The sooner he's back behind bars, the better for all concerned."

Chapter 8

Craig Byfleet was Annette's ex-boyfriend. He lived in a shared apartment in a building that had once housed the local tax office. It was only a five-minute walk from the high street, so I figured I had nothing to lose by dropping by there, on the off-chance I'd catch him in.

I got lucky.

"Yes?" The young man who answered the door was tall—very tall. How do I best describe his look? Charity shop rejects probably does it.

"Hi. Are you Craig Byfleet?"

"Yes?"

"My name is Jill Maxwell. I'm a private investigator. I've been hired by Annette Banks' parents to try and find her."

"What do you mean, *find her*?"

"I take it you didn't know she was missing?"

"I had no idea."

"Would it be possible to come in and ask you a few questions?"

"I am rather busy at the moment."

"Too busy to help to find Annette?"

"I didn't say that."

"I'll only need a few minutes of your time."

"Okay."

He led the way into a large room which served as both kitchen and living room. To my surprise, the room was tidy and spotless.

"Nice place."

"Thanks." He gestured to the leather-effect sofa, which made an unfortunate noise when I took my seat. "I assume you share this place?"

"Yes, but there's no one here at the moment. Just me. No one else."

"Okay."

"My two flatmates are at work. It's my half-day. You're lucky to catch me."

"You said you haven't seen Annette since the split? Have you spoken to her on the phone?"

"No, we haven't spoken since we broke up. If anyone tells you otherwise, they're lying."

"O—kay. Can you think of any reason why Annette might have upped and left? Could it have been because of the breakup with you?"

"No, I wouldn't have thought so. It was all very amicable. I know she was feeling stressed about work and her studies, though. Perhaps she just needed to get away for a while? Did she leave a note?"

"No." I lied.

"Oh? I thought she—err—are you sure?"

"It doesn't appear so. Why?"

"No reason."

"Can I ask why the two of you split up?"

"We'd just grown apart."

"Was anyone else involved?"

"No, nothing like that."

"I've spoken with Annette's flatmate, Gaye. She too mentioned that Annette was feeling a little stressed about work. Any idea why?"

"None. She didn't like to talk about her work."

By the time I left Craig's flat, my *something-doesn't-smell-right*-ometer was beeping. Although he'd answered all of my questions, I came away with the distinct impression that there was something he wasn't telling me. Why had he looked so surprised when I said that Annette hadn't left a note? It was as if he knew I was lying. Had their split really been as amicable as he'd made out? As far as I was concerned, Craig was still a person of interest in this case.

Everyone seemed to agree that Annette's place of work had been a source of some stress to her in recent weeks. Maybe someone there would be able to shed some light on her frame of mind prior to her disappearance.

But that would have to wait until tomorrow because right now I had bigxie business to attend to.

***

I magicked myself over to Candlefield where I'd arranged to meet two bigxies in the Slurp coffee shop. On the wall behind the counter there was a notice advertising a job vacancy.

"Interested, beautiful?" The ugly wizard behind the counter leered at me.

"Me? No."

"Are you sure? You'd do well in here. The punters like a pretty face to look at while they're waiting for their coffee."

"No, but thanks anyway."

"I've not seen you in here before. Are you alone?"

"Actually, I'm supposed to be meeting someone here."

"Who's the lucky guy?"

"Johnny Johnson and Mickey Michaels."

"Two of 'em, eh?" He gave me a wink. "Nice."

This man was making my flesh crawl. "Do you know

them?"

"Course I do. Regulars are Johnny and Mickey. That's them over there — near the window."

"Thanks." I started to walk towards them.

"Hold on!" Mr Creepy called after me. "What about buying something? I'm not running a charity, you know."

"Sorry. I'll just take a bottle of water, please."

"Three-pounds-fifty."

"For a bottle of water? How on earth can you justify that price?"

"It's the production costs." He shrugged. "It's not like it just falls out of the sky, is it?"

I slammed the money onto the counter and picked up the bottle of liquid gold.

"Mickey? Johnny?"

The two bigxies stood up.

"I'm Johnny." He was wearing a shirt, waistcoat and matching shorts — all in a pleasing shade of turquoise.

"I'm Mickey." He was more of a stripes man. Blue and white striped trousers and a red and yellow striped top. A strange combination which shouldn't have worked but somehow did.

"I'm Jill Maxwell." I shook hands with them both, and then we took our seats. "Bob Bobb told me that you'd fallen victim to some kind of sabotage."

"That's right," Johnny said. "It cost me my job."

"Can you tell me what happened?"

"I'd been working for the same vampire for a little over three months. His name was Damien — he was a bit of a narcissist, but otherwise he was okay. The money was good, and he always paid on time. That particular morning, I was due to start my shift at eight as usual."

"You work shifts?"

"Yeah, the work is always shared between at least two bigxies. There's only so many hours you can do at one stretch. I was due to start at eight in the morning and work until four in the afternoon. I was running a little early, so I stopped off in the park across the road from Damien's house. The next thing I knew, it was almost ten o'clock."

"You'd fallen asleep?"

"No. Well, technically, yes, but I'm convinced there was more to it than that. I reckon I must have been drugged. Anyway, when I arrived at Damien's house, he was livid. He'd had to shave himself 'blind' and cut his neck. He didn't give me a chance to explain; he just fired me on the spot. I haven't been able to get another job since."

"And you're sure you weren't just over-tired?"

"Positive. I'd had a good eight hours sleep as usual. Someone nobbled me, and I reckon it's those Mimage scumbags."

"Is that the company that supplies witches and wizards to act as mirror images?"

"Yeah. They're a joke. I saw one of them in action, and he was hopeless. He kept getting his hands mixed up."

"What about you, Mickey?" I said.

"My story is similar to Johnny's except that I did actually make it to work on time, but it might have been better if I hadn't."

"Why, what happened?"

"I worked for a vampire called Robert. That particular day, I'd been feeling a bit off it all morning. As soon as he started shaving, I knew I was in trouble. I just couldn't sync my actions with his. It was a nightmare. He sacked me there and then, and to be honest, I don't blame him."

"And you think someone might have drugged you, too?"

"I'm sure of it, and like Johnny, I reckon Mimage were behind it."

"We aren't the only ones this has happened to," Johnny said. "I've heard of at least another three bigxies that have lost their jobs because of this."

"What do you know about Mimage?"

"They're a relatively new operation. They opened their office about six months ago. I remember laughing when I first heard about them. Everyone knows that witches and wizards can't act as mirror images. No offence."

"None taken. I saw a demonstration of what you guys do, and there's no way I could do it."

"Mimage rely on picking up work from people who are desperate to find a replacement mirror image quickly," Johnny said. "I was told by one of the other bigxies, who worked at Damien's house, that Mimage had contacted him within an hour of me getting the sack. How could they have known about the vacancy so quickly unless they were behind it?"

"It certainly sounds suspicious."

"Will you be able to help?" Mickey said.

"I'll certainly try to find proof of what they're doing. What outcome are you hoping for, exactly?"

"That you get them shut down before they destroy the livelihoods of any other bigxies."

"I'll give it my best shot."

***

My phone rang; it was Grandma.

"I'm ready for you."

"Sorry?" Why did she always have to be so cryptic?

"You said you wanted help with your marketing, didn't you?"

"Yes, but—"

"I have a small window in my busy schedule, so you'd better get down here pronto."

"Couldn't you have given me a little more notice?"

"Do you want my help or not?"

"Yes, but—"

"Then get down here now."

"Where are you?"

"In Ever."

"Which Ever?"

"Whichever what?"

"Not *whichever*. Which Ever?"

"I don't know what you're talking about. It's no wonder your marketing doesn't work if it's as confused as this conversation."

"I meant which shop are you in."

"Why didn't you say so, then? I'm in Ever of course; up on the roof terrace. Hurry up."

I could feel a migraine coming on.

"Hi, Jill." The head Everette, Julie, greeted me at the door. "Your grandmother is up on the terrace. I should warn you that she's been on the cocktails for a while now."

"Great."

The temperature on the roof was at least ten degrees

higher than it had been on the street. I wished Julie had warned me that Grandma was wearing a bathing costume—it might have prepared me a little for the sight that greeted me.

"Would you like one of these?" She took a sip of a green cocktail.

"No, I have to drive. How many have you had?"

"Not enough. I'm celebrating the launch of ForEver Young cream."

"I take it that it was a success, then?"

"What do you think? We can hardly keep up with demand."

"That's all well and good, but what will you do when all the returns come in?"

"What *returns*? What makes you think there'll be any returns?"

"Come on, Grandma. You know as well as I do that the infomercial is a complete con. As soon as people try it for themselves, and realise it doesn't work, they'll all request a refund."

"Jill, Jill, Jill." She tutted. "Will you never learn?"

"What?"

"You've failed to take into account the 'self-delusion' spell."

"The what? I've never heard of it."

"That's because I only invented it a few days before the launch. It's included in every jar of cream sold."

"What does the spell do?"

"It convinces the user that the cream has had just the effect they were hoping for. When they look in the mirror, they see a younger version of themselves."

"That's—err—that's—"

"Genius?"

"I was going to say despicable."

"Thank you. I am rather proud of it. Now, I suppose we should turn our attention to the travesty that is your business. What exactly is the problem that you're hoping my marketing expertise can help you with?"

"I need to find a way of attracting more customers. Preferably paying ones."

"Is there another type? Come and sit down next to me, and we'll get started." She pressed a button on the table next to her.

"What does that do?"

"It summons all of the greatest thinkers in Candlefield."

"Really?"

"Of course not." She broke down in hysterics, and was still laughing when Julie appeared with another green cocktail.

"Did she just buzz you?" I asked.

"Yes. She had that button put in a couple of days ago. I reckon I've lost half a stone, walking up and down the stairs since then."

"That will be all." Grandma took the cocktail and then dismissed Julie with a wave of the hand. "So, Jill, talk me through your current marketing strategy."

"I have a small ad in Washbridge Pages."

"In what?"

"You know. The phone book thingy they deliver to everyone."

"Which everyone throws straight into the bin. How much business does that generate?"

"I'm not exactly sure."

"You must have some idea. Surely, when a new

customer comes to your office, you ask how they heard about you?"

"Sometimes. When I remember."

She sighed. "Any other advertising?"

"Not really. It's mainly word of mouth."

"So, to summarise, you advertise in a publication that virtually no one reads, and have no idea if it generates any business or not?"

"It sounds bad when you put it like that."

"Tell me about your social media presence."

"There's not much to tell."

"You're on Facebook, obviously."

"I'm not, but Winky has a page on Feline Social."

"Your cat?"

"Does that count?"

"What do you think? How about Twitter, Instagram, LinkedIn?"

"I've heard of some of them."

"There's no wonder your business is struggling. How do you think people find goods and services these days? I'll tell you: it's all done online. If your business doesn't have a strong social media presence, you may as well pack up and go home."

"Okay, but I'm not really sure how to go about it."

"Quelle surprise. Fortunately for you, I have two gurus who handle all of my social media."

"Great. Will they sort something out for me?"

"Of course. I'll just tell them to *sort it out*, shall I?"

"Yes, please."

"Give me strength. It doesn't work like that. It's also going to require a lot of input from you."

"But I'm really busy."

"No, you're not. If you were, you wouldn't be here asking for help with your marketing. Their names are Dom and Nic."

"What's the other one's name?"

"I've just told you."

"You said: Dominic. What's the other guy's name?"

"One of them is called Dom. The other's name is Nick."

"Oh, right. I thought you meant—"

"What?"

"Nothing. It doesn't matter."

"I'll get in touch with them and have them contact you ASAP."

"Okay, thanks."

"I think we're done here." She lay back on the sun lounger. "Tell Julie to bring me some crisps up, would you? And none of those awful cheese and onion ones she gave me last time. How am I supposed to attract the gentlemen if my breath smells of onion?"

***

After leaving Ever, I decided to call it a day, and drove home. I'd no sooner parked on the drive than I heard the familiar tooting sound of Mr Hosey's train, Bessie. My instinct was to rush into the house, but seeing as he'd come to the rescue on my wedding day, I figured the least I could do was pass the time of day with him.

"Hello there, Jill." He brought the train to a halt in front of our house.

"Hi. I haven't really had a chance to thank you for helping out the other day."

"My absolute pleasure. In fact, it worked out very well

for me too."

"Oh?"

"I've been inundated with enquiries from couples, hoping to hire Bessie for their big day."

"That's great."

"Sorry, Jill, I'd love to stick around and chat, but I have a meeting with someone who is going to set up an online presence for Bessie: Website, social media, that kind of thing."

"Right, bye then."

If Bessie was about to get a social media presence, then I'd better get my backside in gear and do the same.

Chapter 9

Jack and I were eating breakfast at the kitchen table.
"Don't forget I'm going to be late home tonight," I said.
"Why?"
"You know why."
"I've forgotten," he lied. "Tell me again."
"I have to take Winky somewhere."
"Where?" He grinned.
"You know where."
"I honestly don't remember. Is it to the vet?"
"No."
"Where are you taking him, then?"
"To speed dating, as you very well know."

At that, Jack totally lost it, and almost spat muesli across the room.

"I don't see what's so funny."

"Sorry." He managed to compose himself eventually. "You're absolutely right. There's nothing remotely strange or funny about you taking your cat to speed dating."

"I sometimes regret telling you that I'm a witch."

"I'm so glad you did. If I have a rough day at work today, all I have to do is think about you taking your cat to speed dating, and that's bound to cheer me up."

"I expect you to have dinner ready for me when I get home."

"Of course I will, my sweetness. You'll no doubt be starving after all your cat-chauffeuring duties."

"You'll be laughing on the other side of your face when I turn you into a rat."

"You can't do that. Have you forgotten our no-magic pact?"

"You obviously didn't read the small print, did you? I refer you specifically to the *unless my husband is being a pain in the bum* clause."

"You've just made that up."

"Have I, though? Are you sure about that?"

When it was time for Jack to leave, he said, "You wouldn't really turn me into a rat, would you?"

"Of course I wouldn't."

"Phew. You had me worried there for a minute." He gave me a peck on the lips. "See you tonight."

"I might turn you into a cockroach, though," I said after he'd gone through the door.

"Why are you talking to yourself?"

I spun around to find Grandma standing behind me. "You scared me to death."

"Who are you going to turn into a cockroach?"

"Err — no one. What are you doing here?"

"I came to tell you that I've arranged for Dom and Nick to come and see you this afternoon."

"Couldn't you have phoned to tell me that?"

"I could, but then I wouldn't have got a cup of tea, would I?"

"I have to leave for work in a minute."

"You'd better get the kettle on quick then, hadn't you?"

It was pointless arguing, so I made us both a cup of tea.

"No biscuits?" Grandma said.

"Err — I think I'm out of them."

"Really?" She magicked the cupboard door open. "What are those then?"

"Oh, yeah. I'd forgotten I bought some yesterday."

When I offered her the packet, she grabbed three.

"Steady on. They have to last me all week." I pulled the packet away.

"Don't be so tight-fisted. I've only had a couple."

Hoisted by my own petard.

"You really shouldn't magic yourself here like this. What if Jack had seen you?"

"I'd have used the 'forget' spell on him of course."

"I don't want you using magic on my husband."

"That, from the woman who was thinking of turning him into a cockroach."

Touché.

***

One day, I would wake up and find that my world had normalised, and that all the crazy had disappeared.

Today, however, was not to be that day.

"Mrs V, why are you holding a toy steering wheel?"

"It's the only one I could find." She pressed the little red horn in the centre of the wheel. "I'm not sure where to get a full-size one."

"I wasn't really questioning why you have a *toy* steering wheel, as much as why you have one at all."

"Armi thinks I should learn to drive."

"Really? At your—" I thought better of it when I saw her expression change.

"At my age? Is that what you were going to say?"

"No, of course not. It's just that you've never shown any interest in driving."

"That's true, but Armi seems to think it would be good for me. He said it would open up the world, and I suppose he's right. I could go anywhere."

"Have you booked driving lessons yet?"

"No. Armi wanted to, but I said I'd like to get used to the controls first. I thought I'd start with the steering wheel and then progress to the pedal thingies."

"I assume you'll go for an automatic?"

"Armi said it might be best. What do you think?"

"He may be right. Anyway, I'll leave you to it then." I started towards my office. "Oh, just one thing. If we happen to have any clients—"

"Don't worry, I'll hide the steering wheel under the desk."

"That might be best."

"Have you seen what that nutjob is doing now?" Winky was sitting on the sofa.

"I assume you're referring to Mrs V?"

"Who else? What's with the steering wheel?"

"She's planning on taking driving lessons."

"You can't allow her to do that. The roads are dangerous enough already. I almost lost one of my nine lives the other day on my way back from the Cat Hole."

"What's the Cat Hole?"

"One of my favourite watering holes."

"Did you look both ways before crossing? I know what cats are like for running out into the road."

"I'll have you know that I was on a tiger crossing at the time."

"You mean zebra crossing, don't you? Or pelican."

"I know what I mean. Tiger crossings were here long before those two imposters came along."

"I've never seen a tiger crossing."

"Sure you have. All the crossings used to be orange and

black stripes before someone came along and painted over the orange with that boring white. Then they had the audacity to rename them zebra or ostrich."

"Pelican."

"Whatever. It's a travesty if you ask me. Anyway, you can't let the old bag lady loose on the roads."

"I shouldn't worry about it. She probably won't go through with it."

"Let's hope not. Anyway, onto more important matters. You haven't forgotten you're taking me to speed dating tonight, have you?"

"How could I? You'd better hook up with someone because this is definitely a one-off."

"There are no worries on that score. I expect to come away with at least half a dozen phone numbers."

"All of them attracted by your good looks and modesty, no doubt."

The land-line rang.

"Jill, I have a man on the line," Mrs V said. "I didn't catch his name, but I'm sure he said he was *Sir* something. Shall I put him through?"

Sir? I liked the sound of that. It was about time I started to attract a better class of client. I was tired of dealing with commoners.

"Yes, put him through, please."

"Hasbene here. Can I speak to Mr Gooder or Mr Maxwell?"

"I'm Jill Maxwell. How can I help?"

Just then, I caught sight of Winky who seemed to be giving me a strange look. I ignored him.

"Is Mr Gooder, there?"

"There is no Mr Gooder."

"I'm sure I saw his name on your sign when I was in town the other day."

"There was a mix-up with my new sign. I used to be Jill Gooder but now I'm Jill Maxwell."

"And you're a woman?"

"Err—yeah."

"And a private investigator?"

"That's right."

"I suppose you'll have to do, then. How soon can you come and see me?"

"Could you give me an idea of what it's about?"

"There's no time for that now. I'm due at the polo club in thirty minutes."

"Depending on where you are, I could probably get out to see you this afternoon."

"That won't work for me, I'm afraid. I have croquet straight after the polo. How about Monday?"

"I can do that. Where are you?"

"Hasbene Hall. It's on the North Wash Road. Can we say ten o'clock?"

"Ten's fine."

"I'll see you then. Don't be late. I can't abide tardiness."

"I'll be there."

Winky jumped up onto my desk. "Be careful. Don't swallow that plum!"

"What are you talking about?"

"Why were you speaking in that stupid posh voice?" He laughed, and then mimicked me, "*My name is Jill Maxwell. How can I help?*"

"I did not sound like that."

"Yes, you did. All that *la-di-da* nonsense won't do you any good. As soon as you let the act slip, he'll realise you're as common as muck."

"Remind me again, how are you getting to the speed dating?"

"Just my little joke. No offence meant."

The land-line rang again.

"Jill, it's that horrible Bugle man."

"Okay, put him through, Mrs V."

"Jill, it's Dougal. I'm sorry to trouble you, but I wondered if you'd had the chance to look at the hit-and-run yet?"

"Not yet, Dougal, but like I said, there isn't much to go on."

"I appreciate that, but there's definitely something not right here. Please will you see what you can find out?"

"Okay. I'll get back to you as soon as I can, but I'm not optimistic."

I still hadn't got used to the all-new Dougal Andrews. The death of Donna Lewis had obviously had a profound effect on him. Was it possible that they had been more than just work colleagues?

The hit-and-run was a complete mystery, and I didn't even know where to begin, but then I remembered something. It was a long shot; a very long shot, but still, nothing ventured, nothing gained.

It took a few minutes, but I eventually found the tattered business card, which I'd thrown into the top drawer of my desk. I punched the number into my mobile phone.

"Yes?" The man's voice was just as I remembered it.

"Is that—err—Manic?"

"Manic speaking."

"It's Jill Maxwell. You came to see me recently."

"What can Manic do for you?"

There he went again, referring to himself in the third person.

"I'm working on a rather strange case, and I was just wondering—err—you said that—err—"

"Give me the details."

I told him what little I knew about Donna Lewis' death: That she'd been killed in a hit-and-run in West Chipping, which the police believed to have been caused by joyriders.

"Manic assumes there's more to it than that?"

"Donna's husband is convinced she was murdered because she was working undercover on a big story. The problem is that no one knows what she was working on. This could all be something and nothing."

"What's in it for Manic?"

"Sorry?"

"When Manic finds out what really happened to the woman, what's in it for him?"

"I don't know. I don't normally work with third parties. What do you suggest?"

"I'll take twenty-five percent of whatever fee you make."

"Okay, I guess."

"And remember, Manic will know if you short-change him."

"I would never do that."

"Manic will be in touch."

The line went dead, and I was left feeling like I needed

to disinfect the phone, and take a shower.

***

I had an appointment with Joyce Carmichael, the proprietor of Complete Care, the agency that had employed Annette Banks. Her offices were on West Street, so as I was running a little early, I called in at Kathy's shop first.

"I see you're run off your feet," I said.

"This is the first quiet period I've had all day." She put down the magazine she'd been reading.

"I'll believe you, thousands wouldn't."

"It's true. I had three new customers this morning alone. While I was serving one of them, I caught your grandmother looking through the window—she looked livid."

"Why? You haven't been upsetting her, have you?"

"She thought she could move in next door and take all of my trade, but I'm kicking her backside."

"Good for you." Just then, something caught my eye. "What's this?" I picked up one of the glossy flyers for Mr Hosey's wedding train business. "That's me on there!"

"I assumed you knew. He must have taken the photo when we arrived at the hotel."

"I knew Mr Hosey was pushing his new business, but I didn't realise he was using my picture on his flyers."

"You do kind of owe him. He did come to our rescue that day."

"I guess so, but how come you're handing these out? What's in it for you?"

"I get ten percent of any orders he gets as a result of the

flyers I give out." She pointed to the code on the bottom of the order form. "See that? That tells him the order came from us. Good, eh?"

"I suppose so."

"Pete and I are looking forward to the weekend. No kids and lots of spooky ghosts. Whooo, whooo." She waved her arms around like some kind of lunatic.

"Is that supposed to be an impression of a ghost?"

"Why don't you just admit you're scared?"

"Because I'm not."

"I suppose you don't believe in them?" she said.

"That's where you're wrong. I definitely believe in ghosts, but I don't believe this hotel is haunted. It's just a hoax to get gullible people like you to stay there."

"We'll see. Just don't come screaming to me when you see one."

***

"Thanks for agreeing to see me, Mrs Carmichael."

"No problem, and please call me Joyce. I'm happy to do anything if it helps to find Annette."

"How, exactly, does your business work, Joyce?"

"We provide care assistants to individuals, but mainly to care homes who prefer not to employ their own staff."

"How did you get along with Annette?"

"She's a darling. I wish I had a hundred more like her. Don't get me wrong, most of the people on our books are caring and conscientious, but because of the rapid turnover of staff in this industry, we still get a few who are not really suited to the caring profession. Annette was reliable and never caused me any problems."

"Would it surprise you to know that, in the note she left, she mentioned feeling stressed by her job?"

"Not really. The job can be stressful and upsetting from time to time, but Annette seemed to take it all in her stride. Until recently at least."

"Did something change?"

"She'd been at the same care home for over a year without any problems, but then a few weeks ago, she asked about a transfer."

"Did she say why?"

"No, and I didn't like to push her. I promised I'd try and arrange a swap, but then the next thing I knew, she stopped coming into work. It was only when I contacted her flatmate that I discovered she'd run away. I was very surprised. The least I would have expected from her was a phone call. I do hope she's alright."

"The fact that she left a note is promising. It suggests she left of her own accord."

"That's what I don't understand. If she chose to leave, why are you investigating her disappearance?"

"Her parents think there may be more to this than meets the eye. To be perfectly honest with you, I think they're wasting their money, but if it puts their mind at rest, I guess it'll be worth it."

"I do hope she's okay."

"Just one more thing. Could you tell me the name of the care home where Annette had been working?"

"Sure. It was Washbridge Lakeview Care Home."

Chapter 10

Because of Winky's stupid speed dating thing, I wasn't going to get my dinner until late o'clock. I needed something to keep me going until then, so on my way back to the office, I called in at Coffee Games.

I'd no sooner got through the door than a miniature frying pan came sailing through the air. Moments later, I had to duck to avoid a tiny shovel.

"I take it that it's Buckaroo day?" I said to the young man behind the counter who, in the spirit of the game, was dressed as a cowboy.

"It certainly is. Would you like one?"

"No, thanks. Just a caramel latte, please. Oh, and one of those blueberry muffins."

"Don't you like Buckaroo?" he asked, as a tiny guitar landed on the counter.

"It's alright, but I was more of a Pop-up Pirate kid myself, actually."

"You should have been here yesterday, then. I make a pretty good pirate even if I do say so myself."

Before I could take a seat, someone called my name.

"Jill! Come and join us." It was Betty Longbottom; she was sitting next to Sid.

I shuffled onto the bench seat opposite them.

"Come on, Sid." Betty sighed. "How much longer do you need?"

"I'm not sure where to put it." He had a miniature lantern in his hand, and was trying to decide whereabouts on the mule to place it.

"Do you like Buckaroo, Jill?" Betty said.

"It's okay."

"This is our fifth game and so far, I've won them all."

At that precise moment, Sid put the lantern onto the mule, which immediately kicked everything into the air.

"Five-none!" Betty punched the air. "Loser!"

"I'm going." Sid skulked off.

"He's such a bad loser," said Betty, the ever so gracious winner.

"I haven't seen you since — err — "

"The Grand Opening?" She frowned. "It didn't turn out to be so *grand*, did it?"

"What's happening now with The Sea's The Limit?"

"We're still pressing ahead, but it'll be a while until we can open because we have to wait for the insurance money to come through for the smashed tank. The new tanks are much more expensive than those we had before, but at least they should be safe."

"How did Finn take the soaking?"

"He wasn't best pleased, but luckily for us, he's got other things on his mind. Do you remember the jumper he was wearing?"

"Err — vaguely."

"It was part of his new range of knitwear. I don't suppose you've noticed, but loads of them have popped up around Washbridge. Someone is making knock-off copies."

"That's terrible. Any idea who it could be?"

"No, but I think Finn has his legal people on it."

"Good luck with that." Grandma would run rings around them.

"Sorry?"

"I said — err — I wish them good luck with that. It's despicable what some people will do."

"You never told me that Jack was giving up his job to join you in the business."

"You're referring to the sign, I assume? No, the sign-maker messed up. Jack and I could never work together like you and Sid do."

"To tell you the truth, Jill, I sometimes think it was a mistake for us to run a business together. I love Sid, but he's got no drive. Not like me and you."

"Do you ever see anything of Norman?"

"Occasionally. He's moved in with what's-her-face."

"Tonya, the memory woman?"

"You've met her, then?"

"Many times, but you'd never think so. Every time I went into WashBets, I had to remind her who I was."

"I didn't have you down as a gambler, Jill."

"I'm not, but I sometimes had to go and see her boss, Ryan. He's the boyfriend of Megan Love, our ex-next-door neighbour."

"Tonya has quit WashBets. She's working with Norman in his bottle top emporium now."

"I'm amazed that place is still going. Who would have thought you could make a business out of selling bottle tops?"

"Talking of weird business ideas, have you seen the new place that's about to open, two doors down from me?"

"No, what is it?"

"An internet café." She laughed. "Who in their right mind would open one of those today when almost everyone has the internet on their phone?"

When I left the coffee shop, Betty was still practising her Buckaroo technique.

On my way back up the high street, curiosity got the better of me, so I crossed the road to take a look at the new internet café. It wasn't open yet, but two men were in the process of installing a sign.

"You two don't happen to work for Sid Song by any chance, do you?"

"Nah, these are Rusty Signs."

"Why would anyone buy a rusty sign?"

"That's the boss' name: Rusty."

"Right. That makes more sense."

"I heard that Sid Song had an accident. Do you want a sign making?"

"No, it's okay. Sid is already supplying one for me." At least, I lived in hope that he would.

They each grabbed one end of the sign, and for the first time, I saw what it said: HaveIvers Got Internet For You.

Oh dear.

***

I'd no sooner arrived at my offices:

Beep, beep.

I only just managed to avoid Mrs V, as she came sailing past in her office chair.

"You really should be more careful, Jill," she scolded.

"Pardon me, but I wasn't expecting to find you speeding around the office in your chair."

"I'll have you know that I was well below the speed limit."

"Even so, I'm not sure it's a good idea to ride around the office like that."

"How else am I supposed to practise using the steering wheel?"

"Just be careful. I wouldn't want you to hurt yourself."

"I think I'm beginning to get the hang of it now. Watch me."

I took a few steps back until my back was up against her desk. Hopefully, I'd be out of harm's way there.

"Here goes!" She propelled herself across the room. "Turning right." She turned the toy steering wheel to the right.

I could see what she was trying to do, but then she pushed on the floor with the wrong foot, so instead of turning right, she turned left, straight into the wool basket, which toppled over.

"Are you okay?" I rushed over to her.

"I'm fine. Don't fuss. I just got my legs mixed up, that's all."

"I'm not sure how doing this is going to help with the real thing."

"You may be right. Perhaps I should just concentrate on the pedal thingies and the flasher."

"*Flasher?*"

"You know. The thing which flashes on and off when you turn a corner."

"Oh, right, you mean the indicator."

"That's the one. I think I'll focus on those."

"Sounds like a plan to me."

"How do I look?" Winky said.

I studied him for a moment. "The bow tie is a bit much."

"Do you really think so? What about the jacket?" He did

a little twirl.

"I like the colour, but is velvet really a good idea?"

"I've always thought that velvet says a lot about a cat."

"O—kay. Anyway, I have some visitors coming soon. You can't let them see you dressed like that."

"That's alright. I only wanted to show you. I'll take these off until it's time to go. Who are the visitors?"

"A couple of social media gurus that Grandma has set me up with."

"What? Are you crazy? Why would you waste your time with amateurs when you have a real social media expert right here in your office?"

"That's you, I suppose?"

"Who else? There's nothing this cat doesn't know about social media."

"That's as maybe, but I have to see these guys now that Grandma has arranged the meeting."

"Your loss."

***

Thirty minutes later, two hipsters, complete with cropped trousers and beards, breezed into my office.

"Thanks for coming to see me. I'm Jill."

"Fantastic! I'm Nick."

"Brilliant! I'm Dom."

"Dom an' Nick." I laughed.

They looked totally nonplussed. Trendy they might be, but they obviously lacked the ability to appreciate humour of the intellectual type.

"Would you both like a drink?"

"That would be super." Dom fizzed with enthusiasm.

"I'll have a decaf latte with an extra shot and cream, please."

"A tall, non-fat latte with caramel drizzle for me." Nick stroked his beard.

"Actually, we only have filter coffee. Or tea?"

They exchanged a puzzled look, and then both declined the offer.

"Okay, Jill," Nick rested his elbows on my desk. "Your grandmother told us you don't have any kind of social media presence." He laughed. "I assume she was joking."

"Err—no, that's right. I've never actually got around to it."

"But you have a website, right?" Dom leaned forward now, too; it was beginning to feel like an interrogation.

"Sort of. At least I think it's still there."

"You don't know? What's the URL?"

"I can't actually remember. It was very long. Geo something, I think."

"Oh dear." Dom shook his head.

"Oh dear, oh dear." Nick sighed.

"It's something I've been meaning to sort out for some time."

"No worries, we're here now." Dom looked around the room. "What exactly is it you do, Jill?"

"I'm a private investigator."

"Fantastic!" Nick said.

"Brilliant!" Dom could hardly contain himself. "I'm sure we can do something with that." He took out his phone. "Do you have a magnifying glass you could hold?"

"No."

"Not to worry." He snapped a photo of me. "We can use Photoshop to add one."

"What about a bloodhound?" Nick said. "Do you have one of those?"

"No, just a cat." I pointed to Winky who was lying on the sofa (thankfully, minus the jacket and bow tie).

"Definitely not." Nick pulled a face. "He's much too ugly. No matter, we can add a bloodhound too."

"I'm not sure about the magnifying glass and bloodhound," I said, but neither of them was listening.

"We'll start with a new website, Facebook page, Instagram and Twitter." Dom began to tap notes into his phone. "The rest can follow later."

"That sounds like a lot of work."

"Don't worry. We're going to sort it all out for you."

"What will it cost me?"

"Your grandmother has taken care of that."

"*She has*? Are you sure?"

"Positive."

"Great. So, what happens next?"

"We'll go away and get everything set up, then come back and show you when we've finished."

"I imagine that's going to take some time?"

"With a bit of luck, we should be back to show you what we've done by the end of next week."

"Really? That quick? That's great."

"I thought that went very well," I said to Winky, after they'd left.

"Pah." He snorted. "They didn't impress me."

"You're just annoyed because he called you ugly."

"I wouldn't entrust my social media presence to a couple of kids who can't even buy the right size trousers."

"I'm looking forward to seeing what they come up with.

The only thing that worries me is why Grandma has paid for all of this. She must be up to something."

***

I was ferrying my velvet-jacketed, bow tie sporting cat, across town to the speed dating event. As you do.

"Put your foot down!" he shouted from the back seat. "I don't want to be late."

"Shut it! Think yourself lucky I'm doing this at all."

"That's it!" he called out. "Over there."

"Where?"

"The ballroom. With the big pink sign."

I pulled into the car park of The Roxy Ballroom. "Are you sure this is the place? It doesn't even look open."

"This is it. Let me out."

As soon as I opened the back door, he jumped out, and began to rush towards the building.

"What am I supposed to do while you're in there?" I called after him.

"Wait in the car. It only lasts two hours."

"Do you have to stay that long?" I was wasting my breath because he'd already disappeared around the back of the building.

Annoyed at myself for being such an idiot, I climbed back into the car and turned on the radio. It was going to be a long two hours.

I almost jumped out of my skin when, a few minutes later, someone knocked on the window. The young witch gestured for me to wind it down.

"Hi," she said. "Are you waiting for your cat too?"

"Yeah."

"I saw you from across the road. There's a few of us in the café over there. Do you want to come and join us?"

"Sure." I climbed out of the car.

"I'm Debbie."

"Jill. Nice to meet you."

"Is this your first time?"

"Yeah. Last one too, I hope."

In the café, two tables had been pushed together. Around them, a number of witches and wizards were seated. It turned out that they were all waiting for their cats who were at the speed dating event. It seemed that Winky wasn't the only demanding feline, and I wasn't the only mug in Washbridge.

The two hours flew by much quicker than I'd expected, as we all bemoaned our lot.

"They're out!" Debbie pointed.

Across the road, a number of cats were now in the car park, so we all said our goodbyes.

"See you all next time," Dennis, a middle-aged wizard shouted.

"Not me," I said. "This is definitely a one-off."

"That's what they all say."

"Where have you been?" Winky demanded.

"I was across the road in the café."

"I've been waiting here for twenty minutes."

"Did you come out early?"

"Yeah, it was a dead loss. Full of boring, needy females. Not a looker amongst them."

"Does that mean you won't be coming again?"

"No chance. It was a total waste of my time and sartorial efforts."

"That's a real shame."

***

By the time I'd dropped Winky back at the office and driven home, I was dead on my feet. Even though I'd grabbed a packet of crisps in the café, I was starving, and very much looking forward to the dinner that Jack had promised to have waiting for me.

"I'm home!" I shouted. "I hope dinner's ready because I'm starving. And would you believe it, after all that, the stupid cat didn't even enjoy the speed dating."

Jack appeared, red-faced, in the doorway of the lounge, desperately running his finger back and forth across his throat. "Hello, darling. We have guests."

"Guests?" I mouthed.

"The Makers: Pauline and Shawn. Come and say hello."

I followed him into the lounge where our neighbours were seated on the sofa—they both looked puzzled.

"Hi, you two. This is a nice surprise."

"Hello, Jill." Pauline smiled.

"Did you just say you'd taken your cat to speed dating?" Shawn said.

If there was a good way to talk myself out of that situation, I sure as heck didn't know what it was, so I did the only thing I could, and cast the 'forget' spell.

"I'll go back outside and come in again," I said to Jack while the Makers were still coming around.

"Okay."

Take two.

"Hi, I'm home," I called from the hall.
"Hi, darling. We have guests."

Chapter 11

"Making breakfast for me is the least you can do." I pushed Jack out of bed.

"What did I do?"

"You were supposed to be making dinner for me last night."

"It was hardly my fault that we had guests."

"You invited them in."

"What was I supposed to do? Tell them to get lost?"

"How come all of our neighbours turn out to be nutters?" I yawned.

"The Makers seem alright to me."

"Really? What about all the whack job inventions he told us about?"

"I thought the voice-activated toaster sounded like a good idea."

"What good is a toaster that can only toast one side of the bread?"

"He did say it was still in development."

"And what was that waterless washing machine nonsense?"

"Conserving water has to be a good thing."

"Agreed, but what's the point of a washing machine that shreds your clothes?"

"He said there were a few teething problems."

"Admit it, Jack, the man's a head-case. Pauline seems okay, though. Apart from her choice of partner."

"People say exactly the same thing about me." He grinned.

"Watch it!" I launched a pillow at his head.

"I thought you said we were going in your car today?"

"We were, but then Kathy rang and said we could go in theirs."

"That's not like her. She must be up to something."

"I don't know why you always think the worst of your sister."

"You haven't known her as long as I have."

"How many sausages do you want?"

"Just a couple, like always."

"That'll be three then, will it?"

"Obviously. And make sure the bacon is crispy."

"Do you mean *crispy*? Or do you mean burnt to a cinder like you usually have it?"

"Think charcoal."

"That's what I thought. It'll be nice to have breakfast made for us tomorrow morning."

"Are you sure you still want to go to this stupid haunted hotel? I could call Kathy and tell her you've come down with the lurgy."

"Don't you dare. I'm looking forward to a night away." He started for the bedroom door. "Don't fall back to sleep while I'm making breakfast."

"As if I would."

I didn't feel the least bit guilty about getting Jack to make breakfast because he'd let me down badly the previous night. After a long day, which had included cat-chauffeuring, I'd expected dinner to be waiting for me when I arrived home. Instead, I'd had to entertain the Makers for an hour, and then make do with a takeaway pizza.

***

"They're here!" Jack shouted from the lounge. "Kathy's driving, and it looks like she's got a new car."

"What?" I joined him at the window. "That's why she wanted us to go in their car, so she could show off. It's not five minutes since she bought the last one."

"It's nice."

"How come I haven't got a new car?"

"If the marketing assistance that your grandmother is giving you pays dividends, you'll be able to have a new car soon. Come on, we don't want to keep them waiting."

"What do you think of it?" Kathy said.

"What?"

"My new car, of course."

"Oh, right. I hadn't noticed. It's very nice." I climbed into the front passenger seat next to her; Jack got in the back with Peter.

"Isn't it about time you traded in that old wreck of yours?" Kathy glanced at my car, on the driveway.

"There's nothing wrong with it."

"Nothing that a crusher wouldn't sort out."

"How come you can afford to keep swapping your car?"

"Pete's business is doing really well now, and the shop is doing much better than our best predictions."

"I'll be getting a new car soon, anyway. I'm just waiting until I see the right one." Out of the corner of my eye, I spotted Jack's puzzled expression.

"Are we going or what?" Peter said.

Kathy flicked the indicator (or as Mrs V would have it: the flasher), and off we set. "Haunted hotel, here we come!"

Yay! (Not!)

Two hours later, we were on a road which was little more than a farm track.

"Are you sure it's on this road?" I looked out at a field full of cows.

"That's what the SatNav says." Kathy didn't sound very confident.

"*Your destination is on your right.*" The obnoxious SatNav voice informed us.

"I can't see anything," I said.

"There!" Kathy pointed.

"I still can't see it. All I can see is that building that looks like it's about to collapse."

"That must be it. Look, there's a sign."

"Rat Home Manor Hotel?"

"I think you'll find it's Rathome." Kathy pulled into the car park.

"We can't possibly stay here." I wound down the window to get a better look. "It looks like it might fall down at any moment."

"It's fine." Kathy was already getting out of the car. "It all adds to the haunted hotel atmosphere."

"Jack, Peter." I turned to them. "Tell her this is crazy."

"It'll be okay." Peter got out of the car and joined Kathy.

"Jack?" I implored.

"Come on. It'll be fun."

"Traitor!"

I hoped that once we were inside it might look better. It didn't.

"Welcome to the Rathome Manor Hotel." The woman

behind the small reception desk looked as though she'd just time-travelled from the Victorian era. "I'm Euphemia, but everyone calls me Effie. My husband, Efren, sends his apologies that he can't be here to greet you, but he had to go into town for supplies."

"How far away is the nearest town?" I said.

"Just under twenty miles. We're rather out in the sticks here."

"Do you have electricity and running water?" I was beginning to panic.

"Yes, of course. We have our own generator and there's a well out back."

"A well?"

"Just kidding." She laughed. "We're on the mains."

Kathy kicked my foot, and said in a hushed voice, "Stop showing us up."

"I'll take you to your rooms." Effie came out from behind the desk. "I've put you in adjoining bedrooms on the top floor. We're unusually quiet this weekend—there's just one other couple staying with us. Would you like to follow me?" She led the way up a creaking, winding staircase to the top floor.

"Who would like the Phantom Suite?"

"We'll take that." Kathy took one set of keys from her.

"That leaves the Poltergeist Suite for you two." Effie handed Jack the other set of keys. "I'll leave you to settle in. Dinner is at seven-thirty. If you need anything, just give me a shout." She started back down the stairs. "And look out for the ghosts."

"There's no wonder Kathy got a two-for-one voucher for this dump," I said, once Jack and I were in our room.

"There's nothing wrong with this room." He put the case on the bed. "I've stayed in a lot worse."

"You'd think they could afford to put the heating on, wouldn't you? And, did you hear her say that we're stuck in the middle of nowhere?"

"So? The whole point of coming away was to enjoy the peace and quiet of the countryside, and the experience of a haunted hotel."

"Haunted hotel, my bum."

"I take it you haven't seen any ghosts yet, then?"

"Of course I haven't. I told you—this is all a big con."

"Come on." Jack opened the suitcase. "Help me unpack."

"Do we really have to stay?"

"I'm staying. You can hitchhike home if you want to."

Twenty minutes later, Kathy popped her head around our door. "Settling in?"

"Is it freezing cold in your room too?" I said.

"That's just the ghosts."

"Rubbish. The owners are too tight-fisted to put the heating on. Why don't we go and find a proper hotel in the nearest city?"

"Stop moaning, Jill. Why can't you just enjoy the experience?"

"I'm too cold."

"You're exaggerating as usual. It's a beautiful day."

"Out there, maybe, but it feels like the North Pole in here."

"Pete thought it would be a good idea for us all to go for a walk. It'll give us an appetite for dinner."

"That's a great idea." Jack gushed.

"Walk where to?" I said. "There's nowhere within walking distance."

"According to Effie, there's a public right of way that runs close by the hotel. We'll be able to take in the peace and quiet of the countryside."

"Are you being serious?" I said.

"Yeah, we'll meet you downstairs in ten minutes."

"We'll be there." Jack blurted out.

"Have you lost your mind?" I said, once we were alone. "Why did you say we'd go with them?"

"A nice walk in the countryside will do us both good. You're wound up like a spring—this will help you relax."

"How can I relax? I'll be too busy trying to dodge cowpats."

I was wasting my breath as usual. How was it that whenever Jack and I were with Kathy and Peter, I was always in the minority? I'll tell you why—because my husband always sided with them—he was a traitor. I should have turned him into a cockroach when I had the chance.

What? Of course I'm joking.

To be fair, the countryside around the hotel was beautiful, but by far the highlight of the walk was when Kathy stepped in a cowpat.

"It's not funny, Jill!"

"Sorry."

"Did you see that before I stepped in it?" She looked at me, accusingly.

"Of course not. I'd have said something." Snigger.

"It's probably time we turned back anyway." Jack checked his watch.

"I wonder what we'll be having for dinner." Peter let Kathy put her arm around his neck while she tried to clean the worst of it off her shoe.

"Gruel probably," I suggested. "Made from rats' innards."

"Shut up, misery chops." Kathy was now back on both feet. "You're just scared that you might see a ghost."

"I'll have you know that I've seen more ghosts than you've had hot dinners."

"Really? Well, something tells me that you'll be screaming like a little baby if you see one this weekend."

"We'll see about that."

***

"This 'gruel' looks delicious," Jack said, as the four of us sat down for dinner.

He was right; the roast dinner looked amazing, and as I was soon to discover, tasted even better.

"Good evening, everyone. I'm Efren, but everyone calls me Effie. I'm sorry I wasn't here to greet you earlier, but I had to make my twice-weekly trek into town for supplies. Have any of you encountered our friendly ghosts, yet?"

"Pah," I scoffed, under my breath. That earned me a disapproving look from Kathy.

"Do you really have ghosts?" The question came from the blonde who was seated at the only other occupied table. She was young—no more than twenty-two, and looked like she'd just fallen headfirst into a makeup counter. Her partner, a man at least twice her age, had gravy stains on the collar of his yellow shirt. I could only assume he must have been auditioning for the part of

Colonel Mustard in an upcoming movie. Nothing else would have explained the gold suit and shoes.

"We most certainly do have ghosts," Effie (the male version) said. "You're bound to see Joe and Mo before you leave."

"Joe and Mo?" I laughed, which this time earned me disapproving looks from everyone at my table.

"That's just what we call them," Effie said.

"They're not dangerous, are they?" Blondie looked genuinely scared.

"No, they're very friendly. They won't hurt you, but they might make you jump."

"I'll keep you safe, Kittie." Colonel Mustard put his arm around his younger companion.

Just then, Effie (the female version) joined her husband. "Don't let Effie keep you talking. I wouldn't want your dinner to go cold. There's sticky toffee pudding for dessert, so make sure you leave a little room for that."

By the time we'd finished our meals, I was full to bursting.

"That was amazing," Peter said, as we all made our way upstairs to our rooms.

"That Kittie was a bit much, wasn't she?" I said. "All that giggling?"

"She's young, Jill." Kathy gave me that disapproving look of hers. "It's hard to believe it, but you were young once, too."

"What do you mean: *were*? I'm still young."

"You're twenty-eight going on seventy."

"What was that guy with Kittie wearing?" Peter said.

"He looked like he was about to head out on safari." I

laughed. "I hope they're not on the same floor as us. We'll never get any sleep with that giggle of hers."

"You won't sleep anyway," Kathy said. "You'll be too busy looking out for ghosts."

"Joe and Mo?" I scoffed. "They sound more like a comedy act. I think I'll sleep just fine."

***

I was having the most fantastic dream: I'd been hired to work in the quality assurance department at a custard cream factory.

"Jill!" Jack shook me awake. "Did you hear that?"

"I didn't hear anything." I rolled over. "Let me go back to sleep. I was just about to test a batch of custard creams."

Just then, a scream came from out on the landing.

"You must have heard it this time." He jumped out of bed.

"That's one dream I'm never getting back." I grabbed my dressing gown and followed him out of the door.

Standing there, were Peter, Kathy, Kittie and Mustard. Judging by the look of terror on Kittie's face, she must have been the one who'd screamed.

"What's going on?" Jack said.

"There's a ghost in our bedroom." Kittie pointed to the open door.

"She's right." Mustard, who was now wearing gold pyjamas, put his arm around her. "I saw it too. Go and see for yourselves if you don't believe us."

"Okay, we will." I started towards their room, but then realised I was on my own. Kathy, Peter and Jack hadn't moved. "Aren't you three coming?"

"I don't think we should all go in there," Peter said.

"I'll stay with Pete." Kathy grabbed his hand.

"What about you, Jack?"

"I—err—I'll stay with the others."

"Right. So, let me get this straight. You three intrepid ghost hunters are okay with me going in there by myself, are you?"

Their silence spoke volumes.

Sheesh!

The bedroom was cold, but no colder than ours. I put that down to the skinflint owners rather than the presence of a ghost. After searching the room for a few minutes, I came to the conclusion that I was the only one in there. I was just about to re-join the others when I heard something.

A sneeze.

That was no ghost.

A moment later, there was another sneeze, and then the sound of footsteps. I followed the noise, and put my ear against the wall opposite the bed. Someone was behind there, and I had a sneaking feeling I knew who it was.

"Come out, you two, the game's up." I knocked on the wall. There was no reply, so I knocked again. "You have five seconds to get out here. One, two, three—"

One of the wooden panels slid open, to reveal two figures dressed in white.

"Effie and Effie, I assume."

They removed the sheets from over their heads. "How did you know we weren't real ghosts?" Mr Effie said.

"Let's just say I've had a certain amount of experience

with 'real' ghosts."

"Are you a psychic?" Mrs Effie looked impressed.

"Something like that. Why are you doing this?"

"We were on the verge of bankruptcy. The bookings had all but dried up, but then we came up with the idea of rebranding as a haunted hotel. Business has improved dramatically since then. I know you wouldn't think it judging by how few people are here this weekend, but that's only because we had a last-minute cancellation for a party of eight. What are you going to do? If you post this on the review websites, we'll be finished."

"It's okay. I won't say anything."

"Honestly?" Mrs Effie gave me a big hug. "Thank you so much."

"Jill! Are you okay?" Jack shouted through the door.

"Get back in there." I ushered the two Effies back into the secret passageway. Once they were inside, and the wall panel was closed, I called out, "Help! Please, someone, help me!"

Jack came charging into the room, followed by Kathy and Peter.

"You should see the look on your faces." I laughed.

Chapter 12

It took a while, but I finally managed to convince everyone that there were no ghosts and nothing to worry about. Kittie, in particular, took some persuading, but tiredness eventually overcame her, and she retired to bed with Mustard.

"So?" Jack said when we were back in our room. "Did you really see any ghosts?"

"*Now* you want to know? You didn't seem very keen to come into the haunted bedroom with me."

"I would have, obviously, but I thought it would be better if I stayed outside to look after the others."

"That was very noble of you."

"Come on, tell me, were there any ghosts in there?"

"No *real* ones."

"What do you mean?"

"It's just as I predicted. The whole thing is a not-so-elaborate hoax. It was just the owners, wearing white sheets."

"How come we didn't see them when we came into the room?"

"There's a secret passageway behind the wall. That's how they get in and out of the bedrooms."

"Why didn't you tell the others?"

"I felt sorry for the Effies. From the sound of it, this place was on the verge of bankruptcy before they came up with the haunted hotel idea."

"I always knew that, under that tough exterior of yours, beats a heart of gold." Jack gave me a kiss.

"Don't kid yourself, Buster. I still haven't forgiven you for letting me go into that room alone."

"Is there some way I can make it up to you?"

"There most certainly is, but we'll have to keep the noise down or Kittie will think the ghosts are back."

***

What the — ?

Something had woken me again. Jack hadn't stirred this time; he was still sleeping peacefully. Had I just imagined the noise? Maybe it was just a dream.

Then I heard it again: A scraping sound which seemed to come from out on the landing. This was getting beyond a joke. I'd felt sorry for the Effies, which is why I hadn't dobbed them in to the others. When we'd gone back to bed, I'd foolishly assumed they'd leave off their ridiculous haunting escapades for the rest of the night, but apparently not.

I climbed out of bed and tiptoed out of the room, so as not to disturb Jack. Out on the landing, the noise was much louder, and appeared to be coming from the stretch of wall close to the stairs.

"Hey, you two!" I tapped on the wall. "Knock it off!"

The panel began to slide open, and I was all set to give the Effies a piece of my mind when two ghostly figures appeared. *Real* ghosts this time.

"Oh?" I stepped back. "I wasn't expecting you."

"Sorry if we woke you," the man said. Standing next to him was a woman who gave me a little wave.

"Who are you two?"

"I'm Ras." He gave a little bow. "Short for Rasputin."

"And I'm Cassandra, but everyone calls me Cas."

"Ras and Cas? What are you doing here?"

"We've been here for two-hundred years: first alive and now dead."

"You lived here before you died?"

"That's right. The house was much grander back then, wasn't it, Cas?"

"Much. All of the people who have owned it since then have let it go. It breaks my heart to see it like this."

"Have you ever thought of moving to Ghost Town?"

"We tried it for a couple of months," Ras said. "But we couldn't settle, so we've lived here ever since."

"That's right." Cas nodded. "How do you know about Ghost Town, anyway? And how come you can see us?"

"It's a long story. I'm actually a witch."

"You're not that what's-her-name, are you?" Cas scratched her head. "I read about her a little while ago. Gooder, that was it. Jill Gooder. Is that you?"

"Yes, but I'm Jill Maxwell now. I recently got married."

"It's such a pleasure to meet you, Jill. We'd heard rumours about a sup who could travel to Ghost Town, but we weren't sure whether or not to believe them. What brings you here?"

"I'm here with my husband, and my sister and her husband. Did you know that the owners are now promoting this place as a haunted hotel?"

"Yes." Ras raised an eyebrow. "They're an embarrassment, walking around with those sheets over their heads."

"I just don't get it. If they have a couple of real ghosts in residence, why do they feel the need for this pathetic charade of theirs?"

"Probably because they have no idea we're here."

"Really? How come?"

"We don't like to intrude, so we've always kept ourselves to ourselves. You're the first one to discover us."

"In all of this time?"

"Yes, it was quite a shock when you called to us just now, and even more of one when we realised you could see us. It is nice to make contact with someone else after all this time, though. It can be quite lonely."

"I'm sure it can, but I've just had an idea that might help to alleviate your boredom."

I shared my thoughts with them, and they both seemed enthusiastic about my proposal.

***

The next morning, I was up bright and early.

"What time is it?" Jack managed to open one eye.

"Just gone seven."

"It's too early. Come back to bed."

"I thought I'd take an early morning walk."

"A walk? You? Are you sure you're feeling alright?"

"I'm fine. Go back to sleep. I'll see you at breakfast."

I found the two Effies in the dining room, laying the tables ready for breakfast.

"Morning, you two."

"Morning, Jill. We're really sorry about last night. You aren't going to tell anyone, are you? It would ruin us."

"Don't worry. Your secret is safe with me, but there is something I wanted to talk to you about."

"If you want a refund, I'm sure we can sort—"

"No, it's not that. Do you remember last night when you asked if I was psychic?"

"Are you?"

"Yes, and I've discovered something rather interesting."

"Oh?"

"You obviously don't realise it, but this hotel really is haunted."

"Sorry?" They both looked confused.

"It's true. After you'd left last night, I made contact with two real ghosts who have lived here for more than two centuries."

"How come we've never seen them?" Mrs Effie said.

"Do you believe in ghosts? Either of you?"

"Of course not," Mr Effie said.

"And that's precisely why you haven't seen them. They won't appear to non-believers. After I'd sensed their presence, I did some research on this property."

"We've checked Google ourselves, but weren't able to find much about the history of the place."

"As a registered psychic, I have access to records not available to the general public." How did I make this stuff up? "Anyway, I discovered that this building was once a grand house owned by a couple called Rasputin and Cassandra. I believe it was their ghosts that I encountered last night."

"Do you think they might be prepared to make themselves visible to us?" Mrs Effie said.

"I'm sure they will, but only if you truly believe. I suggest you open your minds to the possibility that ghosts exist. If you can do that, then I'm sure Ras and Cas will reveal themselves to you."

"Ras and Cas?"

"Err—I—err—I'm just guessing that's what they'd have called themselves. Rasputin and Cassandra are quite a mouthful."

"Think about it, Effie." Mr Effie turned to his wife. "If we actually had real ghosts, we'd be at full occupancy every night of the week."

"I'll leave you two to think about it." I started for the door.

"Thanks, Jill. Is there anything we can do by way of a thank you?"

"An extra sausage on my breakfast wouldn't go amiss."

***

"Why don't we resolve this once and for all, right now?" Jack said.

"Are you serious?" Peter laughed.

"Why not? There's no time like the present."

We were almost back at Washbridge, and the two guys were debating who was the better ten-pin bowler. I'd had no idea that Peter used to play regularly before he and Kathy got together. Apparently, he'd won a number of trophies in local competitions.

"How come this is the first I've heard of this?" I turned to Kathy.

"Pete likes to keep his light under a bushel. All his trophies are in the loft somewhere."

"So?" Jack pressed Peter. "Are we going to play today or what?"

"Kathy." Peter leaned forward. "How would you feel about me going to the bowling alley with Jack?"

"It's okay by me. I can drop you there on our way to pick up the kids, but you'll have to make your own way home."

"Great!" Jack said. "Best of five frames?"

"Hold on a minute." I turned around to face Jack. "I don't remember you asking if I minded."

"I know you don't mind, sweetness." He leaned forward and gave me a kiss.

"Just don't sulk if Peter beats you."

"Like that's going to happen." He laughed.

After we'd dropped off the two *big* kids at the bowling alley, Kathy called Peter's mum to let her know we were on our way over to pick up Lizzie and Mikey. When she'd finished on the call, it was obvious from her expression that something was wrong.

"What's up?"

"Lizzie has been a bit off it, apparently."

"Sick?"

"I don't think so. Just very quiet as if something has upset her."

"Why don't I get in the back seat? I can have a chat with her on the drive home, to see if I can find out what's wrong."

"Okay, thanks."

As soon as we arrived at Peter's parents' house, I could see what she meant about Lizzie. Normally, she would have come charging down the driveway, full of beans, and keen to tell us about her weekend. Instead, she walked slowly, head bowed, towards the car. Mikey had no such issues. He was as loud as ever.

"Lizzie, come and sit in the back with me." I held the door open for her.

On the journey home, Mikey talked non-stop to his

mother. That gave me the chance to have a quiet word with Lizzie.

"What's wrong?"

"It's Caroline."

"What's happened? You two haven't fallen out, have you?"

"No, of course not. We're still best friends."

"What is it, then?"

"I think she might be in danger."

"Why?"

"I've been getting messages from her all day."

"What kind of messages?"

"Messages in my head."

"What did they say?"

"Help."

"Just that?"

"Yes. I'm really worried, Auntie Jill."

"Could you have imagined it?"

"No!" she snapped. "I didn't!"

"Are you alright, Lizzie?" Kathy glanced back at us.

"She's okay," I reassured her, and then said to Lizzie, "Sorry. Do you often get messages from her?"

"No, that's why I'm worried. Will you check on her, Auntie Jill? Please?"

"Of course I will. And don't worry. I'm sure everything is okay."

***

When we reached my house, Kathy got out of the car too.

"Did you find out what was wrong with Lizzie?"

"It's nothing. She's just a bit upset about one of her friends at school who's been poorly. I think she's worried in case she gets ill too."

"She never mentioned anything about it to me before we went away."

"It's nothing, I'm sure. She'll be right as rain by the morning."

I waved to Lizzie as they drove away, then I checked to make sure there was no one around before magicking myself over to Ghost Town.

I'd been to Caroline's house before, and I was confident that a quick check with her mother would reveal that everything was okay. The 'messages' that Lizzie had heard were probably no more than her overactive imagination.

I could hear movement inside the house, but when I knocked on the door, there was no answer. I tried twice more, and was beginning to get worried when Caroline's mother came to the door.

"Sorry." She looked flustered. "I was just upstairs."

"I apologise for turning up unannounced like this, and I realise this may sound kind of weird, but I was just wondering if Caroline is okay?"

"She's fine."

"Right, good. It's just that—err—Lizzie has been worried about her. Kids, eh? If I could just say hello to Caroline, I can get back and report that everything's okay."

"She's in bed."

"Is she poorly?"

"No. Just an early night."

"Right, I see."

"I'm sorry, but I have to get back inside. You can tell Lisa that Caroline is okay."

"Right, thanks I—"

She'd already closed the door.

Was it my imagination or had she been acting strangely? She was probably just put out because I'd turned up out of the blue like that.

I started back down the path.

Wait a minute!

She'd called Lizzie, Lisa. A mistake? Surely not because I'd only just mentioned her by name.

Something didn't smell right.

Perhaps Lizzie had been right. Maybe Caroline and her mother were in some kind of trouble. I walked down the road, but then doubled-back and made my way around to the rear of the house. I checked the window, but couldn't see anything, so I tried the door.

It was open.

I'd taken no more than two steps into the kitchen when someone slammed the door closed behind me. I spun around to find a man standing there; he must have spotted me when I'd doubled-back. He'd then unlocked the door to set a trap, which I'd walked straight into. I'd seen this man's face before: Constance Bowler had shown me his mugshot.

"Oswald Mean, I assume?"

"At your service." He grinned with a mouthful of rotten teeth.

"What have you done to Caroline?"

"Is that the little girl? Don't worry. She's okay. She's just a bit tied up at the moment."

"If you know what's good for you, you'll give yourself up now."

"I don't think so." He laughed. "I quite like it here. I plan on staying until things have blown over."

"That could be weeks from now."

"That's okay. There's plenty of food in the freezer. Now, if you wouldn't mind, go through there." He pointed.

Caroline and her mother were both tied to chairs. The poor little mite looked terrified.

"It's okay, Caroline," I said. "You'll be out of here soon."

"You shouldn't make promises you can't keep." Mean pushed me towards a third chair. "Sit down!"

I did as he said, and moments later, I was tied to a chair too.

There we remained while I bided my time. I knew Mean would have to take a leak sometime, and sure enough, just over an hour later, he checked our bindings were still secure, and then disappeared upstairs.

As soon as I heard the bathroom door open and close, I cast the 'shrink' spell to free myself. After reversing that spell, I found a knife, which I used to cut through the ropes that were securing Caroline and her mother.

"Go and phone the police. Ask for Constance Bowler. Tell her that Oswald Mean is here and that I told you to call."

"You have to come with us." Caroline's mother grabbed my hand. "He'll be back down in a minute."

"I'll be fine. Go on. Call Constance. Oh, and Caroline,

will you let Lizzie know you're okay?"

"I'll do it straight away. I don't want her to worry."

And with that, the two of them left.

"I'm starving. Which one of you is going to make me some dinner?" Mean reappeared, saw the three chairs and did a double-take. "What the—?"

There was little wonder he was shocked because he found himself face-to-face with three versions of me—one in each chair.

"Who are you?" he yelled. "What have you done with the others?"

"They've gone, but don't worry, you won't be lonely for long because the police should be here any minute."

He took out a knife and plunged it into the first version of me. His hand and the knife went straight through the apparition. He tried again; this time with the second version of me, but once again the blow found nothing solid.

"Think you're clever, do you?" He snarled. "I've got you now. You're dead meat!"

He lunged forward, but with no more success.

"Whoops!" I laughed.

He spun around to find the 'real' me standing behind him.

"Boo!"

"How did you do that?"

"Just my little party trick."

Before he could attack me, I bound him, hands and feet, with his own ropes.

"Who are you?" he screamed. "*What* are you?"

"Sorry. I should have introduced myself. I'm Jill

Maxwell."

"You're not a ghost!"

"Ten out of ten for observation."

"If you're not a ghost, how can you be here in Ghost Town?"

"Haven't you heard about me? Of course you haven't. Sorry, I was forgetting that you've been locked away for a long time. Never mind. I'm sure Constance Bowler will bring you up-to-date, on your way back to jail."

Chapter 13

It was Monday morning, and I'd just about managed to drag myself out of bed. A shower was normally guaranteed to wake me up, but not this morning. It took three attempts just to get my head through the right hole in my jumper.

"Morning, sweet pea." Jack hurried across the kitchen to give me a peck on the cheek.

"How do you do that?"

"Do what?"

"Spring around like a new-born lamb?"

"I'm feeling refreshed from the weekend break. Aren't you?"

"Does it look like it?"

"I know what will set you up for the week ahead," he said.

"What's that?"

"A nice bowl of muesli."

"Forget it. I'm having a sausage cob. In fact, I might have two."

"You haven't asked me yet." He grinned.

"Haven't asked you what? I'm not awake enough for cryptic clues."

"You haven't asked who won at bowling yesterday."

"I don't need to. You're grinning like a Cheshire cat. If you'd lost, you'd be sulking."

"I never sulk."

"What about that time when I beat you at bowling?"

"That was just a fluke. Hold on, it's only just occurred to me. You must have used magic that day. You did, didn't you?"

"That's for me to know and for you to hope."

***

"Morning, Jill," Mr Ivers shouted.

How was it that no matter what time I set off for work, he was always waiting to ambush me?

"Morning, Mr — err — Monty."

"It won't be long now until the launch of my new business venture. You'll never guess what it is in a million years."

"It wouldn't happen to be an internet café, would it, by any chance?"

"That's amazing. How did you know?"

"I saw them erecting your rusty sign when I was on the high street."

"Catchy name I came up with for the new business, don't you think?"

"Very, and not too dissimilar to the name of your home-movie business."

"I'd rather not talk about that. I'm all about the future. There's no point in dwelling on past mistakes."

"True. I assume you've done your research this time?"

"I don't believe in wasting time on research, Jill. You know what they say about procrastination, don't you?"

"Not really, I haven't got around to finding out yet."

What? Come on. What's the point in all this comedy genius if you're going to dismiss it with a sigh?

Mr Ivers continued, "It's the thief of time, and none of us knows how much of that we have, do we?"

A few hundred years in my case. "Do people actually use internet cafes these days? I don't recall seeing one in

Washbridge for some time. They all closed down several years ago."

"Precisely." He beamed. "With no competition, I'm onto a sure-fire winner this time. I expect them to be queuing around the block."

"I hope you're right. When does it open?"

"The week after next. You will come, won't you?"

"I'll try, but I am rather busy at the moment."

"I've booked a major celebrity to perform the opening ceremony, so there's bound to be a big crowd."

"Who's that?"

"Charlie Barley."

"Not *the* Charlie Barley?"

"None other."

"Err—I realise I should probably know this, but just remind me, who is Charlie Barley?"

"You must remember that TV programme in the early eighties called: Where's My Carrot?"

"How old do you think I am?"

"Sorry, it was probably a bit before your time. It was a monster hit."

"And you say it was called where's my—err—"

"Carrot, yes. It was a kind of game show. There were two teams who had to follow clues to locate the golden carrot. Charlie Barley was the host."

"And it was popular, you say?"

"Absolutely. I was a member of the programme's fan club. I've still got some of the memorabilia. I could show you some time."

"Maybe. What has Charlie Barley been doing since then?"

"Mostly personal appearances, I think. They did launch

a spin-off series called Where's My Onion, but it never caught on."

"Right. Anyway, I should get going."

"Don't forget to get there early for the launch."

"I'll do my best." Wild horses couldn't—you get my drift.

***

I was still half asleep when I arrived at work, but I soon woke up when I walked into the outer office. For a moment, I thought I'd taken a wrong turn and stepped into a disco, but then I realised that the flashing lights were coming from Mrs V's desk.

"Can you switch those off, please?" I shielded my eyes from the strobe effect.

"Sorry, dear. I've switched them off now; you can look up again."

"Let me guess." I glanced at the two disco-type lights on Mrs V's desk. "Are they supposed to be indicators?"

"Flashers? Yes, they are. If I flick this switch, this one flashes. If I flick the other switch, the—"

"I get the idea, but I'm still not sure they'll help with the real thing."

"I hope they do. I wouldn't want to flash incorrectly when I'm driving. By practising like this, I can make sure that when the time comes, I click the right switch when I'm turning right, and the left switch when I'm turning—err—"

"Left?"

"See, that's why I need the practice."

"Have you booked your driving lessons yet?"

"No, but I will as soon as I've mastered these and the pedal thingies."

"Right, well, good luck. I'm going to nip out a little later to see Sir What's-his-face."

She looked me up and down and then frowned her disapproval.

"What's the matter?"

"Your outfit."

"What's wrong with it?"

"Nothing normally, but you are going to see a 'Sir'."

"I thought I looked smart. This is a new top."

"Right, I suppose you'll have to do, then."

And with that ringing endorsement echoing in my ears, I went through to my office.

"Winky, do you think I look smart enough to visit with a 'Sir'?"

"If I can look at a king, I don't see why not."

"Huh?"

"Come on, Jill. What's the point in Adele interweaving all of this clever stuff if you're too thick to pick it up and run with it?"

"Who's Adele? Never mind. This outfit is just going to have to do. Anyway, what are you looking so happy about? I thought you'd still be depressed from the speed dating disaster?"

"I have a blind date."

"How did that happen?"

"An old friend of mine, Rob the Romeo, has set me up. I bumped into him yesterday and told him my sob story about losing my three lady friends. He said he knew just the feline for me. Her name is Crystal. According to Rob, she's hot with a capital 'H'."

"What about her personality?"

"We didn't really get around to that."

Men? They're all the same—human or feline—it doesn't matter. "I hope you don't expect me to take you to your blind date."

"There's no need. She lives locally."

"And when is this *romantic* encounter?"

"Saturday night. Now all I have to do is come up with the right outfit. I was toying with going hipster."

Give me strength!

***

Hasbene Hall had seen better days. Even the gargoyles looked like they wanted to move out. The building, which was located in Hasbene Wood, was surrounded on all sides by tall trees. The little light that made it into the clearing was barely enough to illuminate the dark walls. The Rolls Royce parked out front had a personalised number plate: HASBENE 1.

"Good morning, Madam." The butler who answered the door made the gargoyles look attractive. "You must be Mrs Maxwell?"

"That's right. Jill Maxwell for Sir Hasbene."

"It's actually Sir Arthur."

"Right, sorry." I only just managed to suppress a laugh when I realised that made him A. Hasbene.

"Sir Arthur is in the billiard room. Would you follow me, please?"

Sir Arthur Hasbene was indeed in the billiard room, but the table was set out for a game of snooker.

"Do you play, Mrs Maxwell?"

"I've played a few games of pool."

"You'll soon get the hang of it." He handed me a cue. "I thought we could play a frame first and then talk."

"Err, okay, I guess."

He turned to the butler. "Hastings, you can referee."

"Very well, Sir." He pulled a pair of white gloves from his pocket. He'd clearly come prepared.

"I'll break." Sir Arthur addressed the cue ball.

Once he'd split the pack with his opening shot, I tried to pot a red in the left-hand centre pocket, but missed by a country mile.

Sir Arthur attempted a long pot into the bottom right. The red was set to miss the pocket by a couple of inches until Hastings snatched it from the table and dropped it into the pocket.

"One!" The butler-cum-referee called out the score.

What the—?

"Blue," Sir Arthur lined up his next shot: the blue ball into the middle pocket.

Once again, he was wide of the mark, but just as before, Hastings grabbed the ball and dropped it into the pocket.

"Six!"

Unbelievable.

"I should have warned you that I'm rather good." Sir Arthur was smugness personified. "Although I do say so myself." He walked over to the drinks cabinet and poured himself a large glass of whisky, which he proceeded to down in one go. "Care for a tipple?"

"Not for me, thanks. I need to focus on my game."

"That's never been a problem for me." He sank the next red (with the usual help from Hastings). "I can play just as well with a few drinks inside me."

"Seven!"

"So I see. Perhaps we should talk about what it is you want me to help you with."

"Let me just finish this break first."

I stepped back and watched while he made a series of hopeless shots, all of which ended up in the pockets, courtesy of Hastings and his white gloves. When the break reached sixty-six, Hastings allowed the next shot to miss.

"Drat." Sir Arthur stepped back. "I lost a little concentration there. Care to concede?"

"Yes, you're much too good for me."

"Let's go through to the Long Room."

"Do you still need me, Sir?" Hastings said.

"No, that will be all for now."

The Long Room was certainly long, but a room? Not so much. Anyone else would have called it a corridor because it was narrow and ran from one side of the building to the other.

"Have a seat." Sir Arthur pointed to a red chaise longue.

"Thank you." As soon as I sat on it, a cloud of dust shot out of the seat, and it took several minutes for me to stop sneezing.

"Hay fever?" Sir Arthur had poured himself another large whisky from somewhere.

"No, just a tickly nose. So, if you could tell me what it is you need my help with?"

"Certainly. Something rather tragic has happened."

"Oh?"

"A number of items of my wife's jewellery have gone

missing over the last two weeks. Expensive pieces, you understand." His gaze came to rest on my bracelet. "Not tat."

"Your wife? I didn't realise you were married. Is your wife here today?"

"Geraldine? No, she died a month ago. Didn't I mention that?"

"Actually, no."

I could barely believe my ears. He was apparently devastated by the jewellery theft, but hadn't bothered to mention that his wife had recently died.

"I'm sorry for your loss."

"The jewellery isn't lost. I told you — someone stole it."

"I meant the loss of your wife."

"Oh that? Of course. Anyway, about the jewellery. Do you think you'll be able to find who's behind the thefts?"

"Possibly. Was there a break-in?"

"No, nothing like that. I think it may be an inside job."

"Have you contacted the police?"

"Certainly not. I don't want everyone knowing my business. I assume that whatever you and I discuss is confidential."

"Of course. Do you suspect anyone in particular?"

"I certainly do. Geraldine's sister, Joanne, has been sniffing around a lot recently. I wouldn't put it past her. And then there's Mrs Sykes."

"Who's she?"

"She used to be our housekeeper, but I let her go not long after Geraldine passed away."

"Any particular reason?"

"Gross misconduct. The way that woman spoke to me was simply unacceptable. I'd been wanting to get rid of her for ages, but Geraldine wouldn't hear of it."

"Did your wife leave a Will?"

"What business is that of yours?"

"I just wondered if—"

"There is no Will. She never got around to it."

"Right. Do you happen to have photographs of the missing jewellery, by any chance?"

"I do as it happens. I took them only a few days before they were stolen." He reached inside his jacket pocket. "There you are."

"That should help. It's quite fortunate that you happened to take the photos when you did."

"I needed them for the listings."

"Listings?"

"Yes, I was planning to sell them."

"Don't they have sentimental value for you?"

"I can't spend sentiment, my dear. This house requires a small fortune in upkeep."

Probably not as much cash as his whisky habit, though.

I would normally have stuck around to ask more questions, but being in the same room as Sir Arthur made me feel so dirty that I just wanted to get out of that place.

"When can I expect to hear from you?" Sir Arthur asked when Hastings came to collect me.

"Hopefully within a few days."

"Excellent. Maybe I'll give you a return match when you come back."

"I'll look forward to that."

"How can you do that?" I asked Hastings as he showed me out.

"Do what, Madam?"

"Help him to cheat like that?"

"I'm sorry, Madam, I have no idea what you're talking about."

Back in the car, I took a closer look at the photographs. On the back of each one, someone—presumably Sir Arthur, had written a short description and a valuation. The amounts were eye-watering. If those figures were accurate, the bracelet, ring and necklace were worth a combined value of just under twenty-thousand pounds.

The man had been so loathsome that I'd been sorely tempted to tell him where he could stick his case, but I wasn't in a position to pick and choose my clients. Luther had warned me that if things didn't improve soon, the business would go to the wall. I might not like Sir Arthur (understatement of the year), but he was a paying client, and goodness knows I needed as many of those as I could get.

Chapter 14

After being in the company of that despicable human being, I figured I deserved a treat, so after I'd driven back to Washbridge and parked the car, I magicked myself over to Cuppy C.

It was Monday, so neither of the twins was in the shop. Mindy was behind the counter, and as soon as I saw her, I could tell something was wrong; she looked as though she'd been crying.

"Mindy? What's the matter?"

"I'm okay." She snuffled. "I just have a runny nose."

"Have you been crying?"

"It's nothing."

"It must be something." I glanced over at the cake shop where two assistants were behind the counter. One of them was the new recruit.

"Gloria! Take over in here for a few minutes, would you?"

She seemed surprised that I should be handing out orders, but she came through anyway.

"Come on." I took Mindy's hand. "Let's go and have a seat." I led the way to the table furthest from the counter, so we couldn't be overheard by the staff. Fortunately, the shop was quiet—presumably the sup flu was still taking its toll.

We sat in silence for a few minutes while I waited for Mindy to compose herself.

"Some money has gone missing." She managed eventually. "I didn't take it—I swear."

"When did this happen?"

"Yesterday. The twins weren't here, so I was in charge,

and when I came to cash up, there was sixty-pounds missing."

"Sixty-pounds exactly?"

"Yeah. When the twins find out, they're bound to think I've taken it, and sack me."

"Don't be silly."

"I wouldn't blame them if they did. Not after all the trouble I caused them when I was with Miles. Why should they believe me when I tell them I didn't have anything to do with it?" She wiped her eyes. "The thing is, Jill, I really need this job. I don't know what I'll do if I lose it. And I'll never get another one if people think I'm a thief."

"You're not a thief."

"You believe me, then?"

"Yes. Of course I do."

"Thanks, that really means a lot."

I took out my purse and handed her three twenty-pound notes. "Put this with yesterday's cash."

"I can't take your money."

"It's just a loan until we find out what happened."

"What about the twins? What shall I tell them?"

"There's no reason to tell them anything. I won't mention it."

"Thanks, Jill." She threw her arms around me and began to sob. "No one's ever done anything like this for me before."

"It's okay, but there is something I'd like you to do for me in return."

"Of course." She released her bear hug. "Anything."

"I'm spitting feathers here. Can you get me a latte and a blueberry muffin?"

"Coming straight up."

What? Who are you calling a big softie?

I'd almost finished my coffee and muffin when Alan came through the door.
"Hey, Jill, would you like another drink?"
"No, thanks. Better not."
Once he had his coffee, he came over to join me.
"Aren't you at work today?" I said.
"No, I've got two days off. Pearl sent me out to do some shopping, so I thought I'd treat myself to a coffee."
"How's Lily?"
"Beautiful as ever, and twice as noisy. She seems to have found her voice all of a sudden."
"I'm glad I bumped into you. I was going to give you a call to ask you about your shaving routine."
"Eh?"
"I realise that sounds kind of weird, but I was wondering what you did about the mirror."
"You mean because I have no reflection?"
"Yeah. I understand that a lot of vampires pay for a mirror-image service?"
"That's right. I use the bigxies. They're by far the best."
"You haven't by any chance heard of a service called Mimage, have you?"
"Don't talk to me about those cowboys. I tried them for a while because they undercut the bigxies' price, but I lived to regret it."
"What happened?"
"I don't know if you're aware of this, but Mimage employ wizards and witches to act as mirror images. And, no offence, but they really aren't up to the job. The ones they provided me with were next to useless. I ended up

cutting my face to ribbons. I put up with it for a couple of weeks, but then went back to the bigxies. Why do you ask, anyway?"

"Bob Bobb, who runs the bigxies service believes that Mimage are trying to sabotage his staff. He's hired me to find out if that's true." I finished the last dregs of coffee. "I'd better get going. Give my love to Pearl and Lily."

"Will do."

***

I wanted to check out Washbridge Lakeview Care Home where Annette had worked. From all accounts, she'd been happy there initially, but in recent weeks she'd become more and more stressed. If I could find out what had changed, maybe I'd be a step closer to discovering why she'd decided to disappear.

I'd been in contact with Annette's flatmate, Gaye. She'd given me the name of the woman that Annette had worked alongside at Lakeview. Apparently, Annette had been very impressed with Rita Markham's dedication to the job, and in particular how much she'd cared about the residents of the care home.

"Good afternoon." The woman behind reception at the care home flashed a paper-thin smile. "How can I help you?"

"Would it be possible to speak to Rita Markham?"

"Can I ask who you are?"

"My name is Jill Maxwell."

"Do you have a relative staying with us?"

"No."

"What's your business with Rita, then?"

"I was hoping to talk to her about Annette Banks who used to work here."

"I'm sorry. That won't be possible. Only relatives of residents are allowed in the building."

"Is Rita at work today?"

"I can't give out that information. I'm afraid I'll have to ask you to leave."

"I'd only need a minute of her time."

"Please leave or I'll be forced to call security." She picked up the phone to show she meant business.

"It's okay. I'm going."

I was on my way back to the car when someone shouted, "Wait!" A woman was hurrying across the car park towards me. "I heard you asking about Rita."

"That's right. Do you know her?"

"Yes, I work with her sometimes. I'm Sylvia, by the way."

"Do you know Annette Banks?"

"Not well. I spoke to her a few times, but that's all. She mainly worked with Rita."

"They won't allow me inside."

"So I heard. It never used to be like this. Everything changed when the new owners took over." She glanced around to see if anyone was within earshot. "Rita's in the staffroom on her break. If you go around the back of the building, there's another door there. She'll be able to let you in."

"How will she know I'm there?"

"The staff room is the third window in from this side of the building. If you knock on the window, she'll see you."

"I wouldn't want to get her into trouble."

"You should be okay. Our breaks are staggered, so she's the only one in there at the moment."

"Thanks very much."

The woman in the staffroom jumped when I knocked on the window.

"Can you open the door?" I mouthed.

Moments later, she came to the back door. "Can I help you?"

"Are you Rita Markham?"

"Yes?"

"My name is Jill Maxwell. I've been hired by Annette Banks' parents to look into their daughter's disappearance. Her flatmate, Gaye, gave me your name, and said that you worked with Annette."

"I can't talk here." She glanced nervously over her shoulder. "If they see me talking to you, they'll sack me, and I can't afford to lose this job."

"Could we meet somewhere else?"

"I suppose so. Where and when?"

"Wherever and whenever you like, but preferably sooner rather than later." I handed her a business card. "Call me on my mobile any time."

"I thought you said your name was Maxwell."

"I need to get new cards printed. I got married recently."

Just then, we both heard voices coming from somewhere inside.

"I have to go." She began to close the door.

"Call me, please."

"I will."

Considering Lakeview was supposed to be a *care* home, it was somewhat disconcerting that everyone who worked there appeared to be terrified to talk about the place. The sooner I got to speak to Rita, the better.

***

Back in Washbridge, who should I bump into in the car park but Kathy. She was rubbing at a tiny smear on the driver's door of her new car.

"You can clean mine when you've done there if you like," I said.

"I would if I had a month to spare. When was the last time you actually cleaned that rust-bucket of yours?"

"I'm sure it was this year."

"I'm not. Oh, by the way, I meant to call you yesterday to tell you that Lizzie perked up not long after we got home. One minute she had a face like a wet weekend, and the next, she was as bright as a button."

"That's good. Any idea why?"

"Not a clue. Kids, eh?"

"How come you aren't at the shop?"

"I've left May in charge for an hour."

"I'm *Knott* sure that's a good idea."

"Don't you ever get tired of the childish jokes about people's names?"

"Not really."

"Taking her on was a great idea. It gives me time to spend on more important things."

"Like lazing in bed all morning?"

"If you must know, I've just been to see my accountant. We've been discussing the possibility of my opening another shop, possibly in West Chipping."

"Seriously?"

"Yes, but there's nothing definite yet. We're still running through the numbers. What about you? Are you up to anything interesting today?"

"I'm working on a missing person case, but I haven't made much progress yet. I'm just headed back to the office. Hopefully, Mrs V will have stopped flashing by the time I get there."

Kathy stared open-mouthed at me. "Flashing?"

"Not that kind of flashing, thank goodness. She's planning on having driving lessons, so she's trying to familiarise herself with the controls. She started with the steering wheel, and has now moved onto the indicators, or 'flashers', as she insists on calling them."

"You had me worried there for a minute."

When I stepped into the outer office, there wasn't a flasher to be seen. Instead, Mrs V was behind her desk, knitting. I was just about to ask if she'd given up on the driving when I realised that there was a man seated at the far side of the room. He looked familiar, but I couldn't think why.

"Jill, I told this gentleman I wasn't sure if you'd be able to see him, but he said he'd wait anyway."

"Right." When I looked at him again I realised where I knew him from. He was the manager of Washbridge Park Hotel. "Is everything okay? I paid the final bill last week."

"It isn't about your bill. I remembered that you said you were a private investigator, and I may need your services."

"In that case, you'd better come through to my office.

Would you like a drink?"

"I've already had one, thanks. Your receptionist made me a cup of tea."

"Right."

"She also gave me this scarf."

"Nice choice of colours."

"And these socks."

"You can't go far wrong with black."

Winky was nowhere to be seen, which was just as well. I didn't want my hipster cat to frighten away a potential client.

"I'm sorry, but I don't remember your name." I gestured for him to take a seat.

"Noah Way."

"No way?" I laughed.

He rolled his eyes.

"I suppose you've heard that one before."

"Only a million times."

That was a first.

"What can I do for you, Mr Way?"

"Call me Noah, please. We've had a series of thefts in the hotel over the last week or so, and I'm hoping that you might be able to find out who's behind it."

"Have you talked to the police?"

"I'd rather not. This kind of thing has a habit of getting into the papers, and that would be disastrous for business."

"I assume the thefts are from the hotel rooms?"

"Actually, no. They've all occurred in the bar."

"And this has only just started happening?"

"Yes. I've worked at the hotel for three years, and during that time, I can remember only a couple of isolated incidents. There have been five times that number in the last two weeks."

"Gosh. What exactly would you like me to do?"

"I was hoping that you could work undercover in the hotel, to see if you can spot what's going on?"

"I can do that. Do you think a member of staff might be responsible?"

"I hope not. Most of the staff in the bar and restaurant have been with us for some time. I've always felt they were trustworthy."

"When do you want to do this?"

"The sooner the better."

"How about tomorrow night?"

"That would be great."

Not long after Noah had left, Winky came through the window.

"What on earth are you wearing?" I laughed. "Is that your hipster look?"

"Of course not. Do you know nothing about fashion?"

"I know you look ridiculous in that lumberjack shirt."

"I'll have you know that the YUCCIE look is *the* latest thing."

"YUPPIES? I thought they went out with the eighties?"

"Not YUPPIE. *YUCCIE.*"

"What's a YUCCIE?"

"Young Urban Creatives, obviously."

"And that's how Young Urban Creatives dress, is it?"

"This is just part of the look. I've still got to get the jeans and sandals."

"Are you sure Crystal will appreciate the YUCCIE look?"

"Of course she will. I'm going to knock her dead."
"I hope you're right."

***

When I arrived home, there was a giant toothbrush standing on next door's lawn.

Sad to say, this kind of thing no longer surprised me.

"Hi, Jill." It was Clare.

"I take it you're back on the Con circuit?"

"Yes. We've both recovered from that awful food poisoning. We never did find out what caused it."

"You have to be *berry* careful what you eat these days."

"You're right. It was awful not being able to go to a Con last weekend."

"So, what is this week's Con?"

"DentistCon."

"I should have guessed."

"Hi, Jill." A giant tooth came out of the house.

"Hi, Tony. It looks like you need a filling."

"Can you and Jack come with us this weekend?"

"We'd love to, but we're booked up for the next few weekends."

"Jill!"

When I turned around to see who had called my name, I saw Lucy Locket running up the road.

"Sorry, you'll have to excuse me," I said to the toothbrush and tooth. "I hope you enjoy your Con."

When Lucy caught her breath, she said, "Little Jack sent me. The berry man is here. Jack told me to come and get you while he keeps him talking."

"Okay. Let's get going."

By the time we'd run back to the corner shop, she was almost dead on her feet.

"Lucy, will you go and give Jack the nod so he knows he can let the man leave?"

"Okay."

I waited around the corner of the shop until, a few minutes later, a wizard dressed in a purple suit came out.

"Excuse me!" I stepped out in front of him.

"Yes?"

"I'm looking for Candleberries, and I believe you may know where I can get my hands on some."

"I don't know what you're talking about." He tried to sidestep me, but I was too quick for him, and blocked his way.

"Move!" he yelled.

"Or you'll do what?"

He turned around and started to walk away in the opposite direction, but I grabbed his arm.

"You know that Candleberries are poisonous to humans, I assume?"

"I still don't know what you're talking about."

"That's funny because I have CCTV footage of you selling them in this very shop," I lied.

"I—err—" He suddenly made a bolt for it, but he only got a few yards before I turned him into a puppy. A miniature one.

I ignored his pathetic little bark and dropped him into the pocket of my jacket. Then I made a call.

"Daze, it's Jill."

"Hi, Jill. What's up?"

"There's someone here I think you should meet."

"Who's that?"

"A wizard who's been selling Candleberries in the human world."

"That's a despicable thing for any sup to do. Where is he?"

"I turned him into a puppy. He's in my pocket at the moment if you'd like to come and get him?"

"I'm on my way now."

Chapter 15

"You haven't forgotten that I'm away this weekend, have you?" Jack said, over breakfast.

"Are you? Since when?"

"I've mentioned it at least once a day for the last two weeks, although I don't know why I bothered because you obviously weren't listening."

"That's not true. You know I hang on your every word. Tell me again why you're leaving me here all alone. By myself."

"I'm going on a course about the dangers of social media."

"You don't need to go on a course for that. I know everything there is to know about social media now."

"Since when?" He grinned.

"Since Grandma's gurus came to see me. They're setting me up on Facebook, Twitter and all those other things."

"*Other things*? Such as?"

"You know: Instalink or something."

"Hmm."

"When will you get back?"

"Late Sunday. It's in Norwich."

"What am I supposed to do by myself all weekend?"

"You could clean your car for starters."

"I'm not wasting a perfectly good weekend, cleaning my car."

"You could always go around to Kathy's."

"No chance. I plan on having a chilled-out weekend, and I won't get that around there with the kids."

"What will you do, then?"

"I haven't decided yet. I might pamper myself with a

visit to the spa. Anyway, I'd better get my skates on because there's someone I need to see before I go into the office, and I've got those social media guys coming in later this morning."

Even though I rushed around, Jack managed to get out of the house before me. I was just about to leave when there was a knock at the door.

When I opened it, I was confronted by my worst nightmare: Not one, but two clowns.

"Sorry, Jill, we didn't mean to frighten you," Jimmy AKA Breezy said.

"You didn't."

"You look a little pale." Kimmy AKA Sneezy took my hand in her gloved hand. "Are you sure you're okay?"

"Yes, I'm fine." I pulled my hand away. "I was just on my way to work."

"We won't keep you long." Breezy held up a clipboard. "We're collecting sponsors, and wondered if you and Jack would be interested?"

"Sponsors for what?"

"The weekend after next is national Clownathon day. Clowns all over the country will be performing in the street for up to twenty-four hours. You must have seen it in previous years?"

"I can't say I have. How does it work? Is it so much per hour?"

"Nothing as boring as that." Sneezy laughed. "The payments are all based upon the clownometer."

"The *what*ometer?"

"It measures the number of laughs received."

"O—kay. So, I would be sponsoring you per laugh?"

"That's right. A chuckle only registers as half a laugh, obviously."

"What about a smile?"

"They don't count at all. Can we put your name down?"

"I suppose so. How much are other people sponsoring you for?"

"Your next-door neighbours, Tony and Clare, have gone for ten-pence."

"Per laugh?"

"That's right. Your other neighbour, Mr Ivers, has gone for twenty-pence."

"Well, he did win the lottery. Put Jack down for ten-pence, the same as Clare and Tony."

"Jack?"

"Did I say Jack? I meant us."

"That's great, thanks. We hope you and Jack will come and join in the fun on the day."

"We'll do our best."

And once again, those wild horses would be wasting their time.

***

I'd managed to track down Mrs Sykes, Sir Arthurs' ex-housekeeper. When I'd phoned the previous day, she'd said she was more than happy for me to call around and talk to her.

The neighbourhood where she lived was run-down; the kind of place where even the rats had moved out. Her house stood out because it was the only one which didn't have at least one window boarded up.

She answered almost before I'd knocked, which made

me think she must have been looking out for me.

"Jill?"

"That's right."

"Do come in." She led the way into a small, but beautifully decorated lounge.

"This is a lovely room."

"Thanks. I do the best with what I have. I've just brewed a cup of tea. Would you like one? Or I can do coffee?"

"Tea's fine, thanks. Milk and one and two-thirds spoonfuls of sugar, please."

"You're a woman after my own heart, Jill. You must get the same funny looks as I get when I ask for two and one-eighth spoonfuls. People just don't understand, do they? Biscuit? I have shortbread or ginger nuts?"

"Just the tea for me, thanks."

Mrs Sykes was well past retirement age, but still had a spring in her step, and a contagious laugh.

"Hasbene's a horrible man." She laughed. "I refuse to call him a 'Sir'."

"Had you worked at Hasbene Hall long?"

"Fifteen years, but I wouldn't have lasted a month if it hadn't been for Lady Geraldine. Such a lovely woman. How she ended up with that pig of a husband, I'll never know."

"How did she die?"

"Her heart gave way."

"Had she been ill for long?"

"No. She'd seemed perfectly well right up until she collapsed. I'd always assumed he would go first. If there was any justice in this world, he would have." She took a sip of tea. "I know I really shouldn't say that but it's true."

"How long after Lady Geraldine's death did Sir Arthur let you go?"

"The very next morning. He'd been aching to do it for years, but Lady Geraldine always had my back. I can't say I'm sorry to have left, although I will miss the money. I only have my pension to live on now."

"Do you live here alone?"

"Yes. My Albert ran away with the woman from the tripe shop; that was over twenty years ago now."

"I'm sorry."

"Don't be. I was glad to see the back of him. What about you, Jill? Have you got yourself a young man?"

"Yes. Jack and I got married a couple of weeks ago."

"That's lovely. I hope you're better at picking men than I was."

"You're probably wondering why I asked to see you."

"I figured you'd get around to telling me when you were ready."

"I've been hired by Sir Arthur to investigate the theft of some of his wife's jewellery."

"And let me guess, he thinks I took it?"

"Something like that."

"It's alright, dear. I have nothing to hide. You're more than welcome to search the house if you like."

"That won't be necessary." I took out the photos that Sir Arthur had given to me. "Do you recognise any of these?"

"Yes. They were some of Lady Geraldine's favourite pieces. Was there a break-in?"

"It doesn't appear so. He took the photos because he'd intended to sell these items."

"Do what?" She shook her head in disbelief. "I suppose I shouldn't be surprised, but it's not like he needs the money."

"Have you any idea who might have stolen them? Is there anyone else who had access to the house?"

"Not that I can think of."

"Sir Arthur suggested Lady Geraldine's sister might be responsible. Joanne, isn't it?"

"He did what?" Mrs Sykes threw her arms up in despair. "What is the matter with that man? Joanne is cast from the same mould as her sister. She would never do anything like that."

"Sir Arthur told me that Lady Geraldine didn't leave a Will."

"I wouldn't know about that, but if she had, she would almost certainly have left her jewellery to her sister."

"Is it possible that Joanne knew that, and decided to take it anyway?"

"No, definitely not. She would never take anything that didn't belong to her."

"Okay, well, thank you for your time and the tea."

"My pleasure. It's nice to have company for a change."

By the time I left Mrs Sykes, I was convinced that she'd had nothing to do with the theft. Even though I hadn't spent much time with her, it had been long enough to realise she was a proud and good woman.

***

"Where's the old bag lady?" Winky was on the sofa. "She dead?"

"No, she isn't dead. She's attending the funeral of a close friend of hers."

"Tempting fate, isn't she? If I was as old as her, I'd steer well clear of the graveyard. Someone might mistake her for a corpse and drop her into one of the holes."

"That's a terrible thing to say."

"Why are you laughing, then?"

"I wasn't. I was just clearing my throat."

"If you say so." He glanced at the clock. "Oh no!"

"What's wrong?"

"Don't you realise what time it is?"

"No. What?"

"It's salmon o'clock. And look sharp; I'm starving."

Twenty minutes later, Dom and Nick arrived, coffee cups in hand.

"I hope you don't mind our bringing coffee in with us."

"Not at all."

"We took the liberty of getting one for you." Nick passed me the cup. "It's a quad, non-fat, one-pump, no-whip mocha."

"Right, thanks." I took a sip. "Wow, that's strong!"

"Would you like to see what we've come up with?"

"Definitely. I've been looking forward to seeing it."

Dom took out a slimline, white laptop and put it on my desk, then the two of them moved their chairs so they were seated either side of me.

"First, your new website." He clicked the mouse.

"That's a very large magnifying glass," I said.

"We asked ourselves what said private investigator better than anything else, and we decided it was a magnifying glass."

"Right, okay. And you've put the magnifying glass over a picture of me?"

"Exactly." Dom gushed. "It's so brilliant!"

"Totally fantastic!" Nick said.

"I see what you've done, but the magnifying glass does make my face look kind of—err—fishlike, don't you think?"

"Wait until you see the bloodhound." Dom clicked on the menu.

"How come it's sitting at my desk?"

"We used Photoshop to do that. Isn't it fantastic?"

"I'll show you the other pages." It was Nick's turn with the mouse.

Fifteen minutes later, they sat back in their chairs.

"So?" Dom said. "What do you think?"

"You have a lot of magnifying glasses on there."

"Brilliant, aren't they?" Nick said.

"And a lot of bloodhounds."

"They're so cool."

"Not so much of me, though."

"You haven't heard the best part yet." Nick was bursting with excitement.

"What's that?"

"We managed to secure a brilliant URL for the website."

"Oh? What is it? Jill Maxwell?"

"No, that would be boring."

"Jill Maxwell PI?"

"Look! It's right there." He pointed to the browser window.

"Magnifyingglassandbloodhoundinvestigations.com? That's quite a mouthful."

"Brilliant!"

"Fantastic!"

"But how will anyone know that's me?"

"Just wait until you see what we've done with your social media presence. Are you ready?"

They didn't wait for my reply. Instead, they ploughed on with their presentation, taking it in turns to run through the various platforms: Facebook, Twitter, Instagram and a few others that I can't even remember.

When they'd finished, they both sat back, and looked at me expectantly.

"That's — err — " I was struggling to find the right words.

"Brilliant?"

"Fantastic?"

"I guess so, but what happens now? Do I just wait for the customers to come flocking in?"

"No, this is just the start," Nick said.

"It is?"

"Yes. We've created the platforms, but now the real work starts."

"It does?"

"Yes, and it's over to you now."

"*Over to me*? Right. What does that mean, exactly?"

"A business' social media presence is only as good as the person posting to it."

"And that would be me, would it?"

"Absolutely. You have to start posting straight away."

"Posting what, exactly?"

"It varies from one platform to another," Nick said. "You can update Twitter throughout the day to let people know what you're doing."

"And then post photos of things you're doing or have seen to Instagram," Dom said.

And so it went on. The two guys spent the next thirty

minutes running through what and how I should post to the different social media platforms.

"Any questions?" Dom said.

"Err—does my grandmother do all this stuff?"

"Are you kidding?" Nick laughed. "That woman is a demon. Haven't you seen her Facebook page or tweets?"

"I can't say I have."

"You should take a look. If ever someone knew how to play the social media game, it's your grandmother."

They both stood up.

"Our job is done here," Dom said.

"Yeah." Nick gave me a wink. "It's been a blast."

And with that they were gone.

Winky was sitting in the windowsill, grinning from ear to ear.

"What's amusing you?" I said.

"The thought of you on Twitter. That I've got to see."

"If my grandmother can do it, I'm sure I can."

"You've got a long way to go to catch her up. I just checked, and she has over twenty-thousand followers on Twitter."

"That sounds like a lot. I'm just not sure what sort of thing I should Twitter."

"You don't *Twitter*, you *tweet*. Why not post a status update on your paperclip sorting?"

"Shut up!"

***

I was still trying to work out what my first tweet should be when my phone rang.

"Is that Jill?"

"Speaking."

"It's Rita Markham from Lakeview Care Home. You asked me to ring you."

"Thanks for calling. I'd really like for us to get together for a chat."

"You can't come to my house." I could hear the fear in her voice.

"Okay. Could you come to my office, then?"

"No. Someone might be watching."

The woman was beginning to sound slightly paranoid, but I was prepared to do whatever it took to get a sit-down with her.

"How about meeting in a coffee shop? Could you do that?"

"I suppose so. Where?"

"There's one on the high street called Coffee Games."

"Is that the one that used to be called Triangle?"

"That's the one. I could meet you there in ten minutes if you like?"

"I can't make it this morning."

"How about this afternoon, then?"

"I—err—okay."

"What time?"

"Three?"

"Three o'clock it is. I'll see you then."

When I'd tried to talk to Rita at the care home, she'd been nervous, and now she was absolutely petrified that someone might see her speaking to me. Could this have anything to do with why Annette was so stressed before she disappeared? Hopefully, I'd soon find out.

"There, done it!" I said.

"Done what?" Winky feigned interest.

"Sent my first tweet."

"This should be good. What does it say?"

"I'm on Twitter."

"So, let me get this straight." He grinned. "You've sent a tweet to say that you're on Twitter?"

"That's right."

"Inspired."

Chapter 16

What exactly was I supposed to share on my Instagram account?

Cats! Everyone likes a photo of a cat.

"Winky, come here."

"I'm busy."

"You aren't doing anything."

"I'm contemplating the world and my place in it."

"I just want to take a photo of you."

"Why didn't you say so?" He jumped onto my desk. "Make sure you get my good side."

"I was thinking of something less staged. Something more, I don't know, *cat-like*."

"What do you mean?"

"Maybe you could play with something."

"My yoyo is under the sofa. Shall I get that?"

"Err — no — I meant something that a normal cat would play with."

"*Normal?*"

"I didn't mean — err, I meant — "

"I've still got the helicopter. That might be better?"

Fortunately, at that moment, my phone rang; it was Bob Bobb.

"Jill, are you busy?"

"I am a little. What is it?"

"I wondered if you could pop over. There's something I'd like to show you. It'll only take a few minutes."

"Okay. Where are you?"

"In Slurp coffee shop."

I magicked myself straight over there.

"Back again?" The creepy guy behind the counter flashed me a grin. "The job's still going if you want it." He pointed to the job ad on the wall behind him.

"Sorry, I'm still not interested."

"Jill!" Bob Bobb was seated near the back of the shop. "Thanks for coming over. Can I get you a drink?"

"Not for me, thanks. I can't stay long." I gestured to the man behind the counter. "He's a charmer, isn't he?"

"Driller? He's okay—just a bit rough around the edges."

"He makes my flesh crawl."

"I wanted to show you this." He passed me a copy of The Candle newspaper. "Check out page eight."

I flicked to the page where I found a full-page advert for Mimage.

"It's outrageous!" Bob spat the words.

There was no wonder he was so angry. Even though the advertisement didn't mention them by name, it was clearly a blatant hatchet job on the bigxies mirror image service. Amongst other things, it said:

Tired of your mirror image arriving late?

Tired of your mirror image falling asleep on the job?

If you've been let down by your current mirror image service, maybe it's time to try the new, ultra-reliable Mimage.

"They seem to know a lot about the problems you've been experiencing," I said.

"Of course they do. They're behind all of them. It makes my blood boil."

"Have you seen this?" I pointed to a section of small text at the bottom of the ad. "It says they're recruiting more witches and wizards."

"I'm not surprised. We've lost another four contracts to

them only this week. If things carry on like this, we'll be out of business before the end of the year."

"They're holding interviews this Thursday. I might just go, to see if I can get a closer look at their operation."

"That's not a bad idea. Or I could just go around there and bust heads."

"I know you're angry, Bob, but you mustn't do anything stupid."

"I won't. I promise."

"I have to get back, but I'll keep you posted."

***

I was due to see Rita Markham at three in Coffee Games, but first, Joanne Carling, Lady Hasbene's sister, had agreed to talk to me at my offices. When I heard the door open in the outer office, I assumed it must be her, but I was wrong.

"Mrs V? I wasn't expecting to see you today?"

"The funeral was first thing this morning, so I thought I might as well come in and do half a day. I hope you don't mind my wearing black."

"Not at all. Are you sure you feel up to being here?"

"Yes, I'm fine. I'd rather be busy."

"I'm expecting a visitor soon: A Mrs Joanne Carling. Then I have to go out to meet someone at three."

"Okay. I'll wait until your visitor arrives, and then make us all a nice cup of tea."

***

"Thanks for coming in today, Mrs Carling."

"No problem. After I spoke to you yesterday, I had a phone call from Mrs Sykes. She said you'd been to see her. You can't possibly think that she had anything to do with the theft of my sister's jewellery, do you?"

"Having spent some time with her yesterday, I'm certain she didn't."

"I guess that means that I'm your only suspect?"

"Did you take the jewellery?"

"Wow! You don't beat about the bush, do you? No, I didn't."

"What kind of relationship do you have with Sir Arthur?"

"I can't abide the man—never could. I don't know what Geraldine saw in him in the first place. I tried to warn her off him, but back then, she was besotted. That didn't last long, but by the time she realised what a mistake she'd made, it was too late."

"Did you see your sister often?"

"Not as often as I would have liked. It was usually when he'd gone away for a few days. And, occasionally, we met up in town, but that wasn't often because Arthur kept her on a tight leash; he was incredibly jealous."

"Did he have reason to be?"

"No. Geraldine may have regretted her choice of husband, but she would never have been unfaithful. She didn't have it in her."

"Can you take a look at these?" I took out the photos of the missing jewellery. "Do you recognise them?"

"Yes, I've seen Geraldine wearing those."

"Did she have a lot of jewellery?"

"More than me, that's for sure."

"I understand your sister didn't leave a Will?"

"It's not something people like to talk about, is it? She did bring up the subject once when we were out for coffee, and I could have sworn she said she'd made hers. I told her not to be so morbid, and changed the subject. Maybe, I got it wrong. Perhaps she was just thinking about doing it. Do you mind if I make a suggestion?"

"Please do."

"Have you considered this might be an attempt to defraud the insurance company? I wouldn't put it past Arthur."

"I suppose it's possible, but if that's true, I don't understand why he's hired me. It's just asking for trouble. I will look into it, though."

Just as I had with Mrs Sykes, I came away from my meeting with Joanne Carling convinced that she wasn't the kind of person to have stolen the jewellery.

Two interesting issues had come out of the meeting, though: First, the possibility that Lady Geraldine might have left a Will, but if she had, where was it? And then there was the question of the insurance. Was it possible that Sir Arthur had hired me to give credence to the theft story, and in turn, to strengthen an insurance claim?

"I'm ready," Winky said, as soon as Joanne Carling had left.

"Ready for what?"

"My photo." He held up his helicopter.

"Err — maybe later. I have to go out — I have a meeting in five minutes."

***

"Tweeting? The man behind the counter in Coffee Games was watching me type on my phone.

"Yeah. Just a quick update."

Getting a coffee in Coffee Games – it's snakes and ladders day.

"What can I get for you?"

"A caramel latte and a blueberry muffin, please."

"Coming up. Would you like a snakes and ladders game?"

"I don't have anyone to play with. I'm meeting someone, but they won't be here for another twenty minutes."

"I was just about to go on my break. I'll give you a game until then if you like?"

"Okay. Why not?"

"Great. I'm Jed, by the way."

"Jill."

I found a vacant table next to the window, so I could keep a lookout for Rita Markham.

Jed was setting up the board. "You're not one of those ultra-competitive types, are you?"

"Me?" I laughed. "Of course not. It's just a bit of fun, isn't it?"

Fifteen minutes later, and I was absolutely seething. I'd been within four squares of victory when I'd landed on a stupid snake. Now Jed was only two squares from the winning line. If he threw anything greater than a 'one', he would win.

"Thanks for the game." He grinned. "You were unlucky."

"You haven't won yet."

He threw the dice, which rolled across the table, and was about to land 'six' face-up when, as if by magic, it rolled one more time, and landed 'one' face-up.

"Did you see that? It stopped and then rolled again."

"Unlucky." I grabbed the dice. To win only a six would do. And what do you know, I rolled a six. "I win!" I punched the air.

"I can't believe it." Jed shook his head.

"Them's the breaks."

"I'd better get back to work. Thanks for the game. Shall I leave the board with you?"

"No, thanks. Hang on, though. Let me just take a quick photo."

My first post to Instagram: Hashtag snakesandladderschamp.

Oh, the sweet smell of success.

What? Of course I didn't cheat. How could you suggest such a thing?

"Jill?"

I'd been so excited over my (totally legitimate) victory at snakes and ladders that I hadn't spotted Rita Markham's arrival.

"Hi, have a seat. What would you like to drink?"

"Nothing, thanks."

"Are you sure?"

"Yes, I'd just like to get this over with."

"Okay. As you know, I've been hired by Annette's parents to try and find out where she is."

"What if she doesn't want to be found?"

"If I manage to trace her, and she doesn't want her parents to know where she is, then of course, I'll respect her wishes. I'll just tell them that she's safe and well. That's really all that matters to them. Be honest with me, Rita, do you know where she is?"

"No, I promise."

"But you know why she left, don't you?"

She shrugged.

"Can you at least tell me why she'd become so stressed in the weeks before she disappeared?"

"It's that place!"

"Lakeview?"

"Yes. I used to love working there."

"What changed?"

"Everything."

"Sylvia mentioned that Lakeview had new owners. Is that when things changed?"

She nodded.

"Things can often be difficult when a new owner takes over any business."

"Difficult?" Rita spoke so loudly that she drew looks from the adjoining tables. "I'm not talking about a few minor changes. The whole culture of the place changed, and it's killing people."

"What do you mean?"

"The number of deaths has tripled since they took over."

"Are you sure?"

"Of course I'm sure."

"What exactly are you saying? Do you suspect foul play?"

"Nothing I could prove. Every death has to be certified by an external doctor, and so far, none of them has raised the alarm."

"Could the increase in deaths be no more than a coincidence?"

"No. Definitely not."

"And you think that might have something to do with Annette's disappearance?"

"I wouldn't be surprised."

"Why didn't she just quit? Why take off like this?"

"I don't know."

"And why are you so scared? Has someone threatened you?"

"Sorry." She stood up. "I've told you everything I know. Please don't contact me again."

And with that, she was gone. Rita was clearly convinced that something sinister was happening at the care home, and she was obviously frightened. But of what exactly?

***

I grabbed a snack, and then it was off to Washbridge Park Hotel, to work undercover, to try and catch the pickpocket who had been stealing from guests in the bar.

Noah Way, the hotel manager, met me in reception.

"Is there anywhere in particular you'd like me to sit?" I said.

"Sorry?"

"In the bar? Which table has the best vantage point?"

"You must have misunderstood. I'd like you to work undercover as one of the staff."

"Wouldn't it be better if I just pretended to be a customer?"

"The problem with that is there's a limit to how much

you'd be able to see regardless of where you sat. If you pretend to be a member of staff, you'll be able to cover the whole room without attracting attention."

"What did you have in mind? Shall I play the part of a manager?"

"No, I thought you could work as a glass collector."

"Oh? Right."

"Come with me, and I'll set you up with a uniform."

By uniform, he meant a white, beer-stained apron.

"You'll be working with Jordan." Noah introduced me to a young man who was dressed in an identical apron. "This is the lady I told you about, Jordan. I'll leave you to it, Jill. Jordan will show you the ropes."

"Okay, thanks."

"Are you really a private dick?" The young man said.

"I prefer *investigator*."

"I've never met a real live private d—err—investigator before. What do you want me to do?"

"Just do your job as you would normally."

"Okay, great. How should I let you know if I spot something suspicious? Do we need some kind of secret hand-signal?"

"I don't think that will be necessary. Just come and tell me."

"Roger, will do."

"So, Jordan, what is it I'm supposed to do, exactly?"

"It's dead easy. Just walk around the room and pick up all the empty glasses, and keep a lookout for any drinks that have been abandoned. Be careful, though, don't pick up a drink unless you're sure the customer has left. Sometimes they've just nipped to the toilet; they won't be very chuffed if you've taken their drink while they were gone."

"Okay. Anything else?"

"You have to give the tables a quick wipe. Oh, and if you find any peanuts, will you let me have them? I get hungry of an evening, and the peanuts keep me going."

"Will do."

The evening started quietly enough, but by nine-thirty, the bar was full. The customers were a mix of residents and non-residents.

"You'll have to collect more than that," Jordan said when I returned to the bar with a couple of glasses. He pointed to a tray on which were stacked at least twenty empty glasses.

"I'm worried I might drop them."

"Nah, you'll be fine."

On my next sweep of the room, I stacked more glasses on the tray, but I still kept the number down to manageable levels—I didn't want any accidents.

I was much slower than Jordan, but then I was also keeping one eye on the customers, to see if I could spot anyone acting suspiciously.

I'd been monitoring one particular pint glass for some time. It was still half full but had been abandoned for the best part of an hour, so I was satisfied that its owner must have left. There was just about room on my tray to fit it on.

"Jill!" The voice, which came from right behind me, made me jump. I stumbled over the table, sending the tray flying through the air. I watched, in what felt like slow motion, as the glass emptied its contents onto the lap of a woman dressed in a beautiful ball gown.

"Sorry!" I tried to wipe her dress with a cloth.

"Stop!" She stood up. "You're just making it worse. Where's the manager? I want to speak to the manager."

Fifteen minutes later, I was in the small office behind the bar.

"I'm really sorry, Noah."

"It's alright. I've given her a voucher for a free weekend break at any of the hotels in our group. That seemed to placate her."

Just then, Jordan came into the room. "I'm sorry I made you jump, Jill. I was just trying to tell you about a guy wearing a spotted dickie bow. He's been acting funny."

"Is he still here?"

"He isn't the pickpocket," Noah interrupted. "He's the regional manager. He dropped in unannounced to do a spot inspection. Needless to say, I'll have quite a bit of explaining to do."

"Sorry, boss." Jordan bowed his head.

"It's okay. You can leave us to it now."

"Bye then, Jill."

"Bye, Jordan." I turned to Noah. "Do you want me to get back out there?"

"I don't think there's any point tonight. Not after what happened."

"Shall I come back again tomorrow?"

"Let's leave it for now. No thefts have been reported tonight, so maybe the pickpocket has moved on. I'll only be in touch if any more incidents are reported."

"Fair enough. And, by the way, I won't be charging you for tonight under the circumstances."

Much to my dismay, he didn't argue.

Chapter 17

"How did it go at the hotel last night?" Jack had managed to tear himself away from TenPin TV long enough to join me for breakfast.

"It was a total waste of time. I didn't see any sign of the pickpocket."

"I hope you weren't drunk on duty." He grinned.

"Chance would have been a fine thing. They had me working as a member of staff."

"Doing what?"

"Collecting glasses."

"Oh dear." He laughed.

"What do you mean: *oh dear*?"

"Why do you think I always volunteer to carry drinks around the house? You're a liability when you have to carry more than one cup at a time."

"I think you're mixing me up with Jules."

"It went okay last night then, did it? No accidents?"

"No, well—err—"

"I knew it."

"It wasn't my fault. Jordan crept up behind me and made me jump."

"Who's Jordan?"

"The young guy I was working with."

"How many glasses did you break?"

"None. It's carpeted in there."

"You were lucky."

"Not really. One of the pint glasses was half full, and it landed in someone's lap. She wasn't best pleased."

"Priceless." He could barely speak for laughing.

"It isn't funny, Jack. I was so embarrassed I didn't know

where to put myself."

"At least you were getting paid for your embarrassment."

"Actually, I'm not. The manager had to give the guest a voucher for a free-break, so I felt like I should offer to forego my fee for the night. I thought he might decline, but—" Jack was in hysterics now. "It isn't funny!"

"Sorry, you're right. I just have this image of you depositing half a pint of beer in someone's lap."

"I'm glad you find it so amusing. Let's see if you're still laughing tonight."

"Why? What's happening tonight?"

"Have you forgotten that they're delivering the new bed today?"

"Of course not." He grinned. "We'll be able to give it a thorough test tonight."

"In your dreams, laughing boy."

***

On my way into the office, I phoned Mimage to arrange an interview for a job as a mirror image. The woman on the phone told me they'd been inundated with applications, but that I'd secured one of the last slots available that afternoon.

Mrs V was at her desk; she seemed to be shuffling about on her chair.

"Are you okay, Mrs V? Are you in pain?"

"Of course not, dear. I'm practising with the pedal thingies, but I keep getting them mixed up. Remind me again, is it the one on the left that makes you go faster?"

"No, that's the brake. The one on the right is the accelerator."

"It's all very confusing. Why don't they place them in alphabetical order? 'A' for accelerator, and 'B' for brake — then everyone would remember."

"You should write in and suggest it."

"There's no call for sarcasm, Jill."

"Sorry." I stooped down to get a better look under the desk. "Where did you get those pedals from? You haven't stolen them from Armi's car, have you?"

"Of course not. They're from a couple of my old sewing machines that were gathering dust in the garage."

"I'm glad to see that you're looking a little brighter today."

"I'm just pleased the funeral is behind me. Poor Patricia never should have gone into that care home. I'm sure that's what did for her."

"You don't happen to know the name of the care home where she died, do you?"

"It was Lakeview."

"Oh?"

"What's wrong?"

"Probably nothing. I'm working on a missing person case at the moment; the young woman in question worked at Lakeview. I spoke to one of her colleagues yesterday, and she had some scary things to say about that place."

"What kind of scary things?"

"According to her, the mortality rates have increased dramatically since the new owners took over."

"Do you suspect foul play is involved?"

"It's too early to draw any conclusions. It's quite

possible that the person I spoke to is simply unhappy because of the change of ownership. Could you do some research for me, and see what you can dig up on the new owners of Lakeview?"

"I'll get straight onto it."

"Look out!" Winky screamed at me; he was standing on the sofa.

"What's up?"

"There's a giant spider. It's the size of a rat."

"No, you don't." I scoffed. "Fool me once, shame on you; fool me twice, never going to happen. Do you honestly think I've forgotten about the 'Bob' incident?"

He'd once conned me into believing that I'd inadvertently killed his best friend, Bob the spider. I'd felt so bad about it that I'd given Winky extra salmon. Then I'd discovered that Bob was in fact just a toy spider.

"I'm not trying to scam you this time. This spider is real. There it is! Look!"

An enormous spider scuttled across the room, and there was no doubt in my mind that this one was real. "Make way!" I leapt onto the sofa next to Winky.

"What did I tell you?" he said, without once taking his eye off the spider.

"It's a beast. Where did it come from?"

"I don't know. It was there when I woke up this morning. I haven't dared get down from here since. I'm starving and bursting for a—"

"Try not to think about it."

"That's easy for you to say."

Five minutes later, we were both still watching the scary beast, as it ran back and forth across the floor.

"Jill, did you want a cup of tea?" Mrs V came into my office.

"Be careful, Mrs V!" I yelled.

"Whatever is the matter? Why are you standing on there?"

"There's a giant—" Just then, the spider came out from under my desk. "There! Look!"

Totally unfazed, she picked it up and threw it out of the open window. "I didn't know you were afraid of spiders, Jill."

"I'm not. Of course I'm not." I jumped down from the sofa. "It's just that I could see Winky was terrified, so I got up there to keep him calm."

What? Of course I wasn't scared. Don't be ridiculous.

***

Something was still niggling me about Annette's ex-boyfriend, Craig Byfleet. I couldn't shake the idea that he knew more than he'd admitted.

Another visit was called for.

I'd just left the office when I got a phone call from Noah Way.

"Jill, there were more thefts from customers in the bar last night."

"I thought you said that no one had reported any thefts?"

"They hadn't when you left, but later on, a man came to see me because his wallet had disappeared. Then, this morning, another customer reported his wallet had gone too. He hadn't noticed it was missing last night."

"I don't get it. I didn't spot anyone acting the least bit

suspiciously. Would you like me to have another stab at it tonight?"

"Yes, please, but I don't think you should collect glasses."

"No arguments from me there. Why don't I just pretend to be a customer? I'll make sure I cover all of the room."

"Okay."

"Same time as last night?"

"Yes, please."

"Okay. I'll see you then."

Maybe this would give me an opportunity to redeem myself for the fiasco of the previous night.

***

I was on my way to see Craig Byfleet, and had just stepped out of the lift when, across the landing, he appeared in the doorway of his flat. I was just about to call his name when I realised there was someone by his side: A young woman. Probably one of his flatmates.

Except that he was kissing her.

It was always possible that he was in a relationship with one of his flatmates, but that niggling voice in my head told me otherwise.

Instead of intercepting him, I hid behind a pillar. When he was in the lift, I went over to the flat and knocked on the door.

"Did you forget—?" The woman stopped midsentence when she saw me standing there.

"Hello, Annette."

All of the colour drained from her face. "There's no one here by that name."

She tried to close the door, but I'd already wedged my foot in the gap.

"There's nothing to be scared of. I promise I won't tell your parents where you are if you don't want me to. I just need to satisfy myself that you're okay, and that you're not being held against your will."

She hesitated, but eventually stepped aside and let me in.

"Craig won't get into trouble, will he?" she said, once we were seated in the large living area.

"Not unless he *is* holding you here against your will."

"Of course he isn't."

"Your parents are beside themselves with worry."

"Why? I left them a note to explain why I'd left."

"They don't believe you would have upped and left like that—note or no note. And to be fair, they're right, aren't they? Why are you hiding here?"

"I don't want to talk about it."

"Rita said she thought it might have something to do with the new owners at Lakeview."

"You've spoken to Rita?"

"Yes, she seems to be afraid of something. Are you?"

She broke down in tears. "I don't know what to do."

"Why don't you tell me what's going on? Maybe I can help."

It took a while for her to compose herself, but eventually she managed to tell her story.

"I love that job. Absolutely love it. The residents are all fantastic, but then *they* took over. Sobers*Care*? That's a laugh. They don't know the meaning of the word."

"Rita said there'd been an increase in the number of deaths since they took over? Have they made cutbacks or something?"

"If it was just that, I might be able to live with it. It's much worse."

"What do you mean?"

"They're killing people."

"That's a very serious accusation. I thought every death had to be certified by an external doctor?"

"It does, but the owners are clever. They make sure there's no evidence."

"How?"

"I don't know. I wish I did."

"Have you reported this to anyone?"

"I thought about going to the police, but I knew they'd take one look at the doctor's records, and dismiss me out of hand. That's why I took it to the press."

"I'm back!" The door opened, and in walked Craig, shopping bag in hand. "What's *she* doing here?"

"It's okay," Annette said. "I'm telling her about Lakeview."

"Are you sure about this?"

"Yes, I have to talk to someone."

"You mentioned the press," I said. "Which newspaper did you go to?"

"I didn't. I'd read an article written by a freelance reporter who specialised in uncovering corruption. I contacted her directly."

"Her name wasn't Donna Lewis by any chance, was it?"

"How did you know?"

"Someone asked me to investigate her death."

"That was no accident!" Annette said. "She was murdered."

"You can't be sure of that."

"I am. Donna managed to get a job working at Lakeview. Not under her real name, obviously. The last time I spoke to her, she told me she knew what was going on."

"Did she say what?"

"No. We were going to meet up, outside of work, but she died that same night."

"And that's why you went into hiding?"

"They must have discovered she was a reporter. I was terrified they might know that I was the one who had contacted her. You won't tell anyone I'm here, will you?"

"Of course not."

"Not even my parents?"

"No one, I promise."

"What about Lakeview? Can you do anything about what's going on there?"

"I don't know. Hopefully."

"I know something that might help you. Just before I left, another one of my ladies — that's what I used to call them — almost died too. Her name is Esme Brown."

"She survived?"

"Yes."

"Where is she now?"

"Still in Lakeview. I'm really worried for her safety."

"Do you think she might be able to throw some light on what's happening?"

"Maybe. Donna told me that she planned to talk to her, but she never got the chance."

"That's very helpful. Thanks."

"Will you keep me posted?"

"Of course I will."

Once I was out of the building, I called the office.

"These are the offices of Jill Gooder, err—I mean, Jill Maxwell. How may I help you?"

"It's me, Mrs V. Have you come up with anything on Lakeview yet?"

"Yes. The company that bought it is called SobersCare. The man in charge is Mark Sobers. There have been a few reports in the press about the company. Financially, they're doing spectacularly well. They've bought numerous care homes across the country, and profits have soared."

"Anything else apart from the financials?"

"I was just getting to that. There have been a number of reports showing the mortality rates of residents has increased dramatically since they took over, but all the investigations have found nothing suspicious."

"Right. Okay, thanks for that."

"Jill, there is just one more thing. A number of the reports make a big deal about the business model they use. They offer a one-off upfront payment which they guarantee will cover the resident for the lifetime of their stay, regardless of how long they may live. Apparently, that's very unusual. All of the other companies charge on a monthly or annual basis."

"Interesting. Okay, thanks, Mrs V."

"Will you be coming back to the office?"

"I doubt it. I'm stacked with work, and I have to get home early because our new bed is being delivered."

"I'll see you in the morning, then."

"Okay. Safe driving."

I'd no sooner finished on the call to Mrs V than my

phone rang again.

"Manic has something for you."

"Right?"

"The hit-and-run wasn't an accident. A geezer known as Blood was paid to do it."

"*Blood*?"

"His real name is Jim Grey. Word is, he's skipped the country. Spain probably."

"Do you know who hired him?"

"It took some tracking down because there was a chain of people involved, but Manic got to the bottom of it."

"And?"

"Our agreement still stands? Twenty-five percent of your fee comes to Manic."

"Yes, assuming your information proves to be good."

"Manic's information is always good. The guy you're looking for is called Sobers. Mark Sobers. He's a—"

"It's okay. I know who he is. Thanks for getting in touch."

"Manic expects prompt payment. No extended credit."

Any doubts I'd had as to whether foul play was involved at Lakeview, had been dispelled by Manic's phone call. If Sobers was capable of arranging to have Donna Lewis killed, he was capable of anything.

The name Sobers had rung a distant bell, and now it was all coming back to me. Jack had watched a news feature about the young dynamic entrepreneur. He was being lauded for the remarkable job he'd done in building his highly profitable care home empire. From what I knew now, it appeared that he may have done so by killing off his residents. No other company would dare to offer a one-off upfront fee because they could go bankrupt if their residents lived to a ripe old age. But, if you could guarantee that wasn't going to happen, the proposition suddenly became viable.

The question was: How was he killing the residents without raising suspicions from the external doctors? I might have suspected good old-fashioned bribery, but he had care homes throughout the UK. He couldn't possibly have tried to bribe doctors all over the country without at least one of them speaking out. Something else was happening, but what?

Chapter 18

My phone rang: 'Caller Unknown'.

"It's happened again!"

"Sir Arthur?"

"Another piece of jewellery has been stolen. What are you going to do about it?"

"When did you discover it was missing?"

"This morning. It must have happened overnight. Have you spoken to Geraldine's sister and that Sykes woman?"

"I have, and I'm positive neither of them had anything to do with the thefts."

"Well, someone is doing it. The jewellery isn't just walking out of here by itself, is it? If you don't mind my saying so, I think it's about time you earned your fee, and you can start by spending the night here."

"At Hasbene Hall?"

"Where else? Whoever is responsible for the thefts seems to strike during the hours of darkness. If you're here then, maybe you'll catch them."

"When did you have in mind?"

"Tonight of course."

"Actually, tonight I'm —"

"I'll expect you at eleven o'clock. Don't be late!" He hung up.

No sleep for me tonight, then. I would have to go straight from the hotel to Hasbene Hall.

Oh well, sleep is for wimps, anyway.

***

If what Annette Banks had told me was correct, then

Esme Brown had been remarkably lucky to have survived an attempt on her life. It occurred to me that she might still be in some considerable danger, so the sooner I got to speak to her the better.

There was no chance that they would allow me in to see Esme, but that didn't matter because an invisible person doesn't have to ask anyone's permission.

There were two residential wings in the building: South and North. Fortunately for me, there was a small plaque on each door with the resident's name on it. I worked my way down the South wing with no success, and I was almost at the end of the North wing when I struck lucky: the name on the door was E. Brown.

I didn't want to risk scaring the woman to death, so I waited until the corridor was empty, then reversed the 'invisible' spell, before going into the room.

"Who are you?" The old lady was knitting, in an armchair close to the window.

"I'm sorry to barge in on you like this."

"I'll call security." She reached for the pendant, which hung from the ceiling, and held her finger over a big red button.

"Wait! Annette Banks sent me."

"Annette?" She released the pendant. "Is she alright? I heard she'd gone missing."

"She's fine. I was with her this morning."

"Such a lovely girl. Not like some of the others."

"She mentioned that you'd had something of a nasty turn?"

"*Nasty turn?*" She smiled. "It was rather more than that, dear. I almost popped my clogs."

"Are you okay now?"

"Fit as a fiddle. They can't get rid of me that easily."

"*They*?"

"The people who run this place."

"What happened?"

"I woke up in the middle of the night to find that thing hovering over me."

"What *thing*?"

"A grim reaper. He had a sickle and everything."

"In this room?"

"Yes. Right next to my bed."

"You must have been scared?"

"I was terrified. I thought my time had come."

"What happened?"

"I don't know. I reckon I must have passed out. The next thing I knew, the doctor was here."

"Did you tell anyone what you'd seen?"

"Of course I did, but no one believed me. Just the silly ramblings of an old woman."

"What makes you so sure it was the owners that tried to bump you off?"

"When I'd recovered from the shock, I got to thinking about what had happened. I may be old but I'm not stupid. There are no such things as grim reapers or ghosts or any of those other make-believe creatures. That's when I figured it out. The people who run this place are trying to kill us off. We don't cost them any money once we're dead."

"If that's true, how come you haven't moved out? Aren't you frightened?"

"No. What happened to me is on the record now. If it was to happen again, then more questions would be asked. I can't see them trying it on again in a hurry.

Besides which, I don't have anywhere else to go—no family, you see. Anyway, you haven't even told me who you are?"

"Sorry, I'm Jill Maxwell. I'm a private investigator; Annette's parents hired me to find her."

"You said you were with her this morning. Where is she?"

"With a friend. She's fine, but she's worried about you and the rest of the residents here."

"She has a big heart. Tell her there's no need to worry. We're all okay."

I left Lakeview the same way I'd arrived: invisible.

After speaking with Esme Brown, things were beginning to slot into place. For SobersCare's business model to work, they needed to be sure that the residents didn't live to a ripe old age. Their deaths mustn't look suspicious—in other words, they needed the residents to die of natural causes—such as a heart attack. And what better way to induce a heart attack than extreme shock? Waking up in the middle of the night to find the grim reaper leaning over you ought to do it. Of course, I didn't for one minute think that it had been a real grim reaper. I knew a number of them, including Lester, and none of them would have been seen dead dressed like that.

Esme had been lucky. They must have assumed she was dead when they called in the doctor. By the time they realised their mistake, it was too late.

***

The offices of Mimage were above a unicycle shop

called 'The Wheel One'.

"Welcome to Mimage," the young wizard behind reception greeted me with a lopsided smile. "Are you here for an interview?"

"I am."

"Name, please?"

Drat. I'd given a false name over the phone—what was it?

"Err—Polly White."

"Oh? I have an appointment for a Molly Black at two."

"That's me. Molly Black."

"Right?" That had him confused. "Take a seat, would you?"

A few minutes later, the door behind reception opened, and two witches appeared.

"Thank you for coming in," the older of the two said to the other. "We'll be in touch by the end of the week." She turned to the wizard. "Who's next?"

"This lady here. Molly—err—"

"Black." I stood up.

"Come in, please."

I followed her into a spacious office where the first thing I noticed was a large wooden frame, standing to one side of her desk.

"I'm Gillian Happ. I own Mimage."

"Nice to meet you, Mrs Happ." I offered my hand.

"It's Miss. Please take a seat. Do you know what we do here at Mimage?"

"As I understand it, you provide mirror images to vampires."

"That's right. Both here and in the human world. Would

you be able to work in both?"

"Yes, that wouldn't be a problem."

"Good. How much experience do you have with the 'doppelganger' spell?"

"Quite a bit."

"Excellent. What about mirroring someone else's actions? Is that something you've ever done before?"

"I can't say it is."

"Not to worry. Very few of our applicants have, but they can usually pick it up."

"Great."

"I'd like you to try out for me, so I can see how you cope with it."

"Okay."

She walked over to another door at the back of her office. "Melvin, come through, would you?"

Melvin, a tall, slim vampire, went and stood in front of the frame.

"Okay, Molly. In your own time."

"Sorry?"

"Think of the frame as a mirror. You're going to stand behind it, and provide a mirror image for Melvin. Do you think you can do that?"

"Err—yeah, I'll give it a go." I went and stood behind the 'mirror', took a long look at Melvin, and then cast the 'doppelganger' spell so I looked just like him.

"That's a good start," Gillian said. "Let's see how you handle the mirror-imaging. Take it away, Melvin."

Oh dear! I had no idea that trying to mirror someone else's movements could be so difficult. Put simply: I was useless. I moved the wrong arm or leg several times. And once, when Melvin turned his head one way, I turned mine the other.

Over Melvin's shoulder, I could see Gillian, and I felt sure she was about to give me my marching orders, but then her phone rang.

"I told you not to call me today. I'm interviewing all day. Yes, I know. You'll get your money, Driller. Now, leave me alone." She slammed down the phone. "Okay, I've seen enough. Thank you, Melvin."

After Melvin had left the room, Gillian turned to me.

"You need a bit of work, but I think you'll get there. When can you start?"

"Err — next week?"

"Excellent. Leave your number with Casper on reception, would you? We'll be in touch with all the information you'll need."

"Great, thanks."

My gob was well and truly smacked. I'd been completely hopeless as a mirror image, and yet, she'd been happy to sign me up. No wonder the service provided by Mimage was so woeful.

In the end, though, my visit had proven to be worthwhile, if only for what I'd overheard of her telephone conversation.

***

Jack and I arrived home within a few minutes of one another.

"What are you typing?" he said.

"I'm just sending a tweet about the new bed. I'll take a photo of it when it arrives and put it on Instagram."

"Are you sure potential clients will be interested in that kind of thing?"

"According to Dom and Nick, people like to know about the person behind a business."

"Who's Dominic?"

"Not Domin—never mind. Look! It's here."

The Forty Winks van came down the road and pulled up outside our house.

"Daze? I didn't realise you'd be delivering it."

"I'm not. I just came along for the ride. To be honest, I needed to get away from Laze for a while. He's doing my head in."

While Daze and I were talking, Jack led the delivery men upstairs.

"How's the hunt for the slumber fairies going?" I said.

"It isn't. We'll give it a couple more days, and if we've still drawn a blank, we'll give it up as a bad job. I was convinced we were onto a sure thing this time. Where else are the slumber fairies going to find so many beds in one place?"

"Hold on! Beds, pickpockets—I'm such an idiot!"

"Jill?"

"I think I know where your slumber fairies are."

"You do? Where?"

"Can you come with me now?"

"I suppose so."

"Great. I'll explain on the way there."

Just then, Jack came back out of the house.

"Daze and I have to go, Jack."

"Where?"

"I'll explain in the morning."

"Won't you be home tonight?"

"No, I was going to tell you. I have to stay at Hasbene Hall tonight."

"What about the new bed?"

***

Daze and I took my car.

"When the hotel manager told me that he'd been having problems with pickpockets, I should have put two and two together."

"A hotel? Of course. There are plenty of beds there. Which one?"

"Washbridge Park—where Jack and I were married. I worked undercover there last night, but I didn't see anything suspicious, but then I'd only been watching the customers. It never occurred to me that I should be looking out for fairies."

"Even if you'd known, you'd have been hard-pressed to catch them at work. They're really tiny."

"If they're so small, how do they manage to lift a wallet?"

"They work in teams. What's the plan, Jill?"

"I'm not sure. I can hardly tell the manager we want to look for fairies, can I? Hang on, I've had an idea, but I'm not sure you're going to like it."

***

"Jill?" Noah Way looked surprised to see me. "You're remarkably early."

"There's a reason for that. Do you remember my husband, Jack?"

"Of course."

"He's a policeman, and he was able to pass on some information that leads me to believe the pickpocket is actually hiding in the hotel."

"Here? How?"

"He's known as Jock the Lock. As well as being a pickpocket, he's a master lock picker. I have reason to believe that he's hiding out in one of your vacant rooms."

"Shouldn't we call the police?"

"Jack's aware of what I'm doing and is fine with it," I lied. "There's no need to involve the police until I'm sure Jock is here. Do you have a master key and a list of all your vacant rooms?"

"Yes, of course. I'll just get them for you. Do you want me to accompany you?"

"No need. I'm used to dealing with characters like this one."

"Okay." He didn't argue; in fact, he looked quite relieved.

"Jock the Lock?" Daze laughed when I pulled her out of my pocket. "I don't know how you come up with them."

"I've had lots of practice."

"Can I get back to full-size? It creeps me out being this small."

"Sure." I put her on the floor, and then reversed the spell.

"There's a lot of fluff in your pocket." She sneezed. "Where should we start?"

"We'll just have to work our way through this list of vacant rooms."

Twenty minutes later, we'd still seen no sign of the

slumber fairies.

"Maybe I was wrong about this." I sighed.

"How many rooms are there left on the list?"

"This one and two more." I opened the door, and Daze led the way inside.

I wasn't optimistic, but this time, when she checked the bed, she gave me the thumb's up, and beckoned me over. There, under the duvet, was a row of teeny, tiny fairies, all fast asleep.

"They look so cute," I whispered.

"Don't let their looks fool you." She took a clear plastic tube from her pocket, and before I could ask what she was going to do, she'd already scooped up the fairies and dropped them into it.

That woke them up, and they began to thump the plastic with their tiny fists.

"I'll take this lot back to Candlefield." Daze popped the top on the tube.

"Not just yet. The manager is going to expect me to bring out Jock the Lock."

"How are you going to—" Her words trailed away as the penny dropped.

"You caught him, then." Noah took one step back. He obviously didn't want any part of the thug who was handcuffed to me.

"I'm innocent." Daze was doing a fine job of playing Jock the Lock. "I ain't done nothing."

"That's what they all say."

"Thanks very much, Jill," Noah said.

"My pleasure."

"Forget what I said about your bill for the other night.

Send it to me and I'll make sure it's paid straight away."

"Will do."

"Oh, and you'd better charge me something for the time you spent here today."

"Actually, rather than do that, how about you let me have one of your vacant rooms tonight. I'll only need it until about ten-thirty."

"Sure, no problem. Tell the receptionist to give me a call when you get back."

Once we were out of sight of the hotel, Daze reverted to her real self.

"Thanks for your help, Jill."

"No problem. You made a good Jock."

"Thanks. I've done a little amateur dramatics in my time."

"I can tell."

Chapter 19

I had to be at Hasbene Hall for eleven o'clock. Once there, I'd be expected to stay awake for the rest of the night. That's why I'd asked Noah Way if I could have a room at Washbridge Park Hotel. At least that way, I'd be able to get some shut-eye in the early part of the evening. I suppose I could have gone home, but as we'd just taken delivery of the new bed, I didn't think I'd get much rest there.

I was in the hotel room, in bed, by seven. I wasn't sure if I'd sleep because it was still light, but I did, and the next thing I knew, the alarm on my phone woke me up. Unfortunately, instead of feeling invigorated for the night ahead, I felt like death warmed up.

"You're late!" Sir Arthur met me at the door of Hasbene Hall.

"It's only just turned eleven."

"It's five-past."

"Sorry."

"And what happened to your hair? You look like you've been pulled through a hedge backwards."

He was right; I hadn't had time to do anything about my bed-hair.

"Where do you want me to spend the night?"

"The bedroom."

"No chance!"

"I meant Geraldine's room. That's where all her jewellery is kept." He led the way up the winding staircase, and along a wood-panelled corridor. "This is it. I'm just across the way there if you need me."

"Okay. Goodnight, then."

The bedroom was beautifully furnished with an antique four-poster bed as its centrepiece.

I was still only half awake, and the temptation to climb into the bed was almost overwhelming, but that would have been a mistake. Instead, I took a seat at the dressing table on which stood a large jewellery box. If the thief returned tonight, he would be in for a shock when he found me waiting there for him.

Time dragged. It felt as though I'd been there for hours, but when I checked my watch, it had only just turned midnight. My eyelids were heavy, and I came close to nodding off several times.

This was hopeless—I had to do something to wake myself up.

I began to walk circuits of the room, past the bed, past the dressing table and then past the wardrobes. Every time I came close to the bed, it was like a magnet drawing me to it. Maybe, I should just put my head down for a couple of minutes? No! I had to stay awake. But it looked so comfortable and inviting.

"What the—?" I woke up to find myself on the bed, in darkness.

How had I allowed myself to fall asleep? I didn't remember getting onto the bed or turning the light out. But I couldn't worry about that now because there was someone in the room with me, and it sounded like they were over by the dressing table.

"Hey, you!" I switched on the bedside lamp.

"You can see me?" The ghostly figure of a man stared at me in disbelief. "How?"

"Never mind that. Why have you got your hand in that jewellery box?"

He pulled it away. "I wasn't stealing anything."

"Really? Just like you didn't steal the other pieces that have gone missing from this room?"

"I can explain."

"Save it for the Ghost Town police. I'm sure Constance Bowler would love to hear your fairy stories."

"How do you know about Ghost Town? You're not a—"

"Ghost? No, I'm a witch, but I'm able to travel back and forth between here and GT."

"I had no idea that sups could do that."

"As far as I know, I'm the only one who can."

"Don't call the police, please. At least hear me out first."

"I'm all ears."

"Is it okay if I sit down?" He pointed to the armchair.

"Help yourself."

"My name is Roland Rook, but everyone calls me Rooky."

"That's very interesting." I tapped my watch. "But time's a ticking by."

"Sorry. I run a business, based in Ghost Town, called GT-Fairshare. We help ghosts to reclaim property that was owned by them when they were alive."

"Let me get this straight. You take property from the human world and re-unite it with the original owners who are now in GT?"

"More or less, but I can't do it for just anyone. Only for those who have been treated unfairly when they were alive."

"How come your clients don't simply come and get it themselves?"

"You obviously aren't familiar with the GT laws regarding importing property from the human world?"

"Not intimately, no."

"It's forbidden other than by licensed operators."

"And that's you, I suppose?"

"I'm one of them. It isn't easy to become licensed; there are only four of us in the whole of GT. We have to prove we have a rigorous vetting system to ensure we only take on deserving clients."

"I assume that your current client is Lady Geraldine Hasbene."

"Yes, but she actually prefers to be called Gerry, these days."

"And she asked you to recover her jewellery?"

"Not all of it; just six pieces in total. I've only managed to find four of them up to now."

"That's a very good story — better than I was expecting."

"Thank you."

"That doesn't mean I believe it. For all I know, it could be a pack of lies."

"I promise you it isn't."

"I'd like to speak to her myself."

"Who? Gerry?"

"Yes."

"I couldn't possibly allow that. Client confidentiality and all that."

"I'd better give Constance Bowler a call, then."

"Hold on! I suppose I could make an exception just this once. When did you want to speak to her?"

"Right now's good for me."

"Now? But I don't know — "

"Oh, well. If you can't, you can't." I took out my phone.

"Wait! I'll ring her now." He made the call. "Gerry? It's Rooky. No, I haven't. There's been a slight hiccup. There's someone here who'd like to talk to you. No, not your husband. Actually, I don't know her name." He turned to me.

"Jill Maxwell."

"It's Jill Maxwell. She's a witch but she can—. You have? Really? Okay then, we'll be with you shortly." He ended the call. "We can go over there now."

"Why can't she come here?"

"She hasn't travelled back to the human world yet. It would take her ages to get the hang of it."

"Fair enough. We'll go over there."

"Gerry said she'd read about you in the newspaper. She sounded quite excited about meeting you."

***

"You'll have to excuse the mess in here, and the state of my hair." Gerry was busy pulling out her curlers. "I wasn't expecting guests. I was just about to make myself a cup of tea. Would you both like one?"

"That would be nice, thanks." My mouth felt like the bottom of a budgerigar's cage. "Milk and one and two-thirds sugars, please."

"Why don't I make it?" Rooky volunteered.

"Thank you, Rooky. Shall we sit, Jill?" She gestured to the dining table.

"Thanks for seeing me at such short notice."

"My pleasure. It's not every day I'm visited by a celebrity."

Hey, did you hear that? She just called me a celebrity.

Gerry continued, "I can't wait to tell them at the bridge club that I had the famous Jill Maxwell over for tea. I almost didn't recognise your name, but then I remembered reading recently that you'd got married."

"My wedding was reported over here?"

"It wasn't a news article. I think your parents put a piece in the paper about it."

"Really? I had no idea."

"Rooky said you wanted to speak to me?"

"Yes. I've been hired by your husband, Sir Arthur, to find out who's been stealing the jewellery."

"Oh dear. I was hoping he might not notice if only a few pieces went missing. I should have known better. I'll go and get them, so you can take them back to him."

"Before you do that, Gerry, will you tell me what motivated you to hire Rooky. Was it so you could wear the jewellery here in GT?"

"No." She laughed. "I'm not the same person now. I wouldn't be seen dead wearing that stuff."

Seen dead? She was a ghost!

"Then why?"

"In my Will, I left everything I owned to my sister. Everything except for six pieces of jewellery that I bequeathed to Mrs Sykes. I figured she'd be able to sell them. She doesn't have much money so losing her job must have hit her hard."

"Wait a minute. I understood from your husband that you hadn't left a Will?"

"I most certainly did. Arthur knew where it was."

"I don't understand. Why didn't he say so?"

"Why do you think? The man always was greedy."

Rooky brought the tea through and joined us at the

table.

"Why didn't you just get Rooky to recover the Will?"

"When Gerry first approached me, that's what she asked me to do," Rooky said. "But I had to tell her it wasn't possible because I'm only licensed to bring over valuables. I'm not allowed to touch legal documents."

"That's when I came up with the idea that Rooky could bring over the jewellery," Gerry said. "I thought I could sell it, and then he could take the cash to Mrs Sykes. I just feel so sorry for her."

"She's a nice woman."

"You've met her, then?"

"I have. And your sister."

"I'll go and get the jewellery for you."

"Don't bother. I have a better idea."

***

Before returning to the human world, I called in on Constance Bowler.

"Jill? To what do I owe this unexpected pleasure?"

"I'm actually after a favour."

"How can I help?"

After she'd heard me out, she agreed to do what I asked.

"When will you need them to be there?" she said.

"Hopefully, I won't, but if you could prep them to be ready for tonight at midnight, that would be great."

"Will do."

Back at Hasbene Hall, I found what I needed, then set the alarm on my phone, and lay down on the bed. At six-thirty, I went downstairs to find Sir Arthur.

"Morning, Sir Arthur."

"Any news?"

"Nothing, I'm afraid. There was no sign of the jewellery thief."

"Blast!"

"Don't worry. I know a few fences in this area. I'll ask around to see if any of them have seen your jewellery."

"*Fences*? Are you talking about the type of person who sells on stolen property? Aren't they a rather unsavoury bunch?"

"They can be, but then I meet a lot of unsavoury people in the course of my work. I'll be in touch if I find anything."

***

After I'd got back to Washbridge and parked the car, I called Jack.

"Morning," he said through a yawn.

"Are you still in bed?"

"Of course not. I've just had my shower."

"How was the new bed?"

"It would have been better if you'd been in it with me, but yeah, it's very comfortable. How was your night?"

"Quiet. Nothing happened." I didn't have the energy to try to explain the intricacies of GT-Fairshare.

"What are you going to do now? Are you coming home to catch up on your sleep?"

"I'm too busy. I'll be okay—I did manage to catnap. I'm just on my way to get a gallon of coffee before I nip into the office. I just wanted to speak to my darling husband first."

"That's very sweet. I'll see you tonight, then."

"About that. There's a good chance I'll be late in."

"How late?"

"Very."

"How come?"

"Do you remember that Sobers guy you were fawning over the other day?"

"The care-home millionaire?"

"That's him. It turns out our Mr Sobers has been a naughty boy."

"What's he done?"

"It's a long story. I'll update you when it's all sorted."

"Okay. Take care. Love you."

"Love you, too. See you tonight."

Coffee Games was as quiet as I'd ever seen it, but then it was still early o'clock.

"Morning." The young woman behind the counter yawned.

"A large cappuccino, please. Do you do breakfast cobs?"

"Of course. Sausage, bacon or egg?"

"Yes, please."

"Which?"

"Can I have them all on one cob?"

"Sausage, bacon and egg?"

"Yeah. Make it two eggs."

"Okay."

"Thanks."

"Draughts?"

"There is, isn't there?" I shivered. "Is there a window

open somewhere?"

"Not that kind of draft." She held up a board game. "It's draughts day."

"Right, no thanks. I'm more of a chess player myself."

What? It's true. You should see my Benoni Defense.

I'd no sooner taken my seat than who should appear, but—yes, you guessed it.

"Morning, Jill."

"Mr Ivers? What are you doing here?"

"Monty."

"Sorry, Monty. How come you're here at this time of the morning?"

"I'm meeting the shopfitters in a few minutes. Anyway, I might ask you the same question. How come you're here so early?"

"I was working all of last night, so I didn't make it home."

"It sounds like you could do with a business partner. You should have taken me up on my offer when you had the chance."

"Oh well. My loss, I guess."

"Would you like a quick game of draughts while I wait for my men to turn up?"

"Actually, I was just about to leave."

"Really?" He glanced at the full cup of coffee in front of me.

"Yeah." I downed the lot in one go. "Got to run. Bye."

Mrs V hadn't yet arrived at the office.

"What are you doing here at this time?" Winky stretched. "Bed catch fire?"

"I've been hard at it all night."

"Yeah." He grinned. "I heard you'd had a new bed delivered."

"Very funny. I've been working on a case as it happens. Anyway, how do you know about the bed? Have you got our house staked out or something?"

"I might have."

"That's just creepy. By the way, have you finalised your outfit for the blind date with Crystal?"

"Yes, I told you. It's all about the YUCCIES now."

"If you say so."

"How's the social media coming along?"

"Like a dream. I'm tweeting, and posting to Facebook and Instagram like a pro."

"Good for you."

Mrs V arrived an hour later.

"Jill? How come you're here at this hour? Bed catch fire?"

"Winky's already cracked that joke."

"Sorry?"

Whoops! That's what comes of speaking when I'm still half-asleep.

"I said—err—Jinky's already cracked that joke."

"Who's Jinky?"

"She works in Coffee Games. I've been working on a case all night, so I called in there to grab a coffee before I came into the office."

"That's an unusual name."

"It is, but then she's an unusual woman."

"I see. Would you like a cup of tea?"

"Not just yet. There is something I would like you to do,

though."

"What's that? It doesn't involve the cat, does it?"

"No. I'd like you to do some more research on Mark Sobers. Specifically, I'd like to know the address of the office where he's based, and if you can find it, his home address."

"Have you made any progress on the Lakeview case?"

"Nothing to report yet, but I'm getting closer."

"Okay. I'll see what I can find on our friend, Mr Sobers."

"Jinky?" Winky laughed.

"It was the best I could come up with. I sometimes forget that no one else can hear you speak."

"More's the pity. People would benefit from my words of wisdom."

"When was the last time you said anything wise?"

"Didn't I recently update you on the state of modern day youth culture? If it wasn't for me you'd know nothing about YUCCIES."

"And what a loss that would be."

Chapter 20

I had my fingers crossed that no one had taken the job at Slurp coffee shop.

"You're always in here, darling." The slimeball behind the counter treated me to another one of his creepy smiles. "I reckon you must fancy me."

"Is that job of yours still available?" I gestured to the notice on the wall behind him.

"Sure is. Fancy it, do you?"

"What's the pay?"

"Minimum wage, of course."

"I was hoping for more."

"Minimum wage is all I can afford. Interested?"

"Maybe. What are the hours?"

"Six till one. Five days a week. You had any experience?"

"Yeah, I've worked in a coffee shop before."

"You'll still have to have a trial first, so I can make sure you know what you're doing. If that goes okay, you can start next week."

"Fair enough. When can I take the trial?"

"No time like the present. What's your name, anyway?"

"Jill."

Five minutes later, I was kitted out in an apron, and standing behind the counter.

"Do you know your way around one of these?" He pointed to the coffee machine. It wasn't exactly the same model as the one in Cuppy C, but it was very similar.

"Yeah."

"Good. Off you go, then. I'll be watching you."

"By the way, what should I call you?"

"Sir." He laughed. "Nah, call me Driller. Everyone does."

"How did you get that nickname?"

"I worked on the oil rigs before I bought this place."

The door opened, and in walked two vampires.

"Your first customers." He nudged me. "Don't forget, I'll be taking notes."

Truth be told, I hadn't exactly excelled behind the counter at Cuppy C, but after I'd finished serving the two vampires, Driller gave me the thumbs up. Clearly, his standards were much lower than those of the twins.

"Just one more thing," he said. "If you get any bigxies in here, I'll serve them."

"Why's that?"

"Because I'm the boss and I said so."

"Right, okay."

Over the next couple of hours, we had a mixed bag of customers: a dozen or more witches, slightly fewer wizards, five or six vampires, three werewolves, and a couple of elves. I was beginning to think I might not see a bigxie when two of them walked in together.

"I'll take this." Driller practically pushed me out of the way. "Hi, guys. Your usual?"

They both nodded.

I watched him like a hawk, but I spotted nothing unusual in the way that he prepared their drinks. Maybe my theory had been wrong.

The following hour saw a similar mix of customers. The next bigxie to come through the door was alone.

"Yes, Sir." Driller had once again brushed me aside. "I don't think I've seen you in here before?"

"No, this is my first time."
"Just finished work, have you?"
"I wish. I'm just about to start my shift."
"No rest for the wicked. What can I get for you today?"
"A flat white to go, please. Make it a large one."
"Coming right up."

Once again, I watched him very closely, and this time, I saw him drop a pill into the cup. As soon as the bigxie was out of the door, I took off the apron, and pushed it into Driller's hands.

"What's this? You haven't finished your trial yet."
"Sorry, I've changed my mind about the job."
"Timewaster!" he called after me, as I hurried out of the shop.

Once outside, I spotted the bigxie, and set off in pursuit.

I deliberately bumped into him. "Whoops! Sorry." Just as I'd hoped, he dropped the cup, and spilled its contents all over the pavement.

"Watch where you're going!"
"Sorry, I'm such a klutz." I hurried away.

When I was out of sight of the coffee shop, I called Bob Bobb.

"Bob, it's Jill. I think I may have some good news for you."
"What's that?"
"I'm in Candlefield now. Could we meet up?"
"Of course. I can be at Slurp in twenty minutes."
"Not in Slurp. Would you mind if we met up in Cuppy C?"
"Sure."
"Okay, see you soon."

As it was such a beautiful day, I decided to take a short detour through Primrose Park. The flowerbeds were in full bloom, and in the centre of the park, children were cooling down by running through the jets of water that shot up from beneath their feet.

That's when I spotted two familiar figures: Miles Best and Cuppy C's newest recruit, Gloria Huss. I hid behind a tree, so they wouldn't see me, but I needn't have bothered because they only had eyes for one another.

***

"Hi, Mindy." I glanced around the shop. "No Amber?"

"Didn't you know? She and Pearl have both gone down with sup flu."

"Oh dear. Who's looking after Lily and Lil?"

"Your aunt Lucy has got both of them."

"Poor Aunt Lucy. She'll be run ragged. It's a good thing they have you to hold the fort here."

"They might not think so when they find out that money is going missing."

"Has it happened again?"

"Yes. Twenty-pounds yesterday. I'm going to have to tell them this time."

"Don't do that just yet."

"What else can I do? I can't afford to make it up from my own purse."

"I understand that, but listen: On my way here, I walked through Primrose Park, and you'll never guess who I saw in there. Your old boyfriend; he was with Gloria."

"Gloria Huss?"

"None other."

"And they were *together*?"

"Very much so."

"Do you think she took the money?"

"I'd bet my life on it. We both know what Miles is capable of, and he's obviously still bitter at the way you dumped him. He must have put her up to it."

"I'll kill him!" Mindy was livid.

"All in good time. First, though, you need to catch her in the act."

"Don't worry. I will."

Just then, Bob Bobb arrived.

"What would you like to drink, Jill?"

"Something cold, please."

"Ice tea?"

"That would be great."

Once we had our drinks, we found a free table away from the other customers.

"What have you found out, Jill?"

"I know who is nobbling your operators."

"Who?"

"Driller."

"You must be joking." He laughed. "Driller has always been a good friend to the bigxies."

"That's what he'd have you believe, but in fact, he's being paid to spike the drinks of bigxies who are on their way to work."

"How can you be sure?"

"I got lucky. While I was being interviewed at Mimage, I heard the owner talking to someone on the phone. They were chasing her for money she owed them."

"So?"

"I heard her refer to the caller by name: Driller."

"Are you sure?"

"One-hundred percent certain. I was only a few feet away."

"But you can't know the money owed was for nobbling bigxies. It could have been for anything. Maybe he supplies food and drink to Mimage."

"Trust me, Driller is your man. I applied for a job at Slurp. In fact, I've just come from there. He gave me a trial to see if I was up to the job, and one of his first instructions to me was that he wanted to serve all the bigxies."

"But I've been in there numerous times and nothing has ever happened to me."

"He's very clever about who he selects. He only picks the bigxies who aren't regulars, and who are on their way to work. I bet if you check with Johnny and Mickey, you'll find out that they called into Slurp on their way into work on the day they were nobbled. It's ingenious when you think about it."

"I'll ask them. I still can't believe Driller would do something like this."

"I saw him with my own eyes. He spiked the coffee of a bigxie just now."

"Are you absolutely sure?"

"Positive. I told Driller that I didn't want his job, and then I chased after the bigxie to make sure he didn't drink the coffee."

"I'm going to kill him!" Bob stood up.

"Wait!" I grabbed his arm. "That might make you feel better, but it will also land you behind bars. Sit down."

"Sorry. What's the plan, then?"

"You have to speak to the police. Tell them what I've just told you, and try to persuade them to run a sting operation."

"How do you mean?"

"They'll need to get one of their people inside the shop, preferably seated at a table close to the counter. Once the undercover police officer is in place, send in one of your operators—it should be someone who has never been in Slurp before. When Driller makes small talk with him, make sure your operator says he's just on his way to work. As soon as Driller has served the coffee, the police can pounce. It should be easy enough for them to confirm that the drink has been spiked."

"Wouldn't it be better if you spoke to the police?"

"Not really. Maxine Jewell isn't a fan of mine. If she knows I'm involved, she'll want nothing to do with it."

"Fair enough, but don't you want to be involved in the sting itself?"

"Much as I'd like to be there to see Driller get his comeuppance, he might smell a rat if I showed up again. Just make sure you let me know how it goes."

"Don't worry. I will. Thanks, Jill."

***

Mrs V had come up trumps with her research into Mark Sobers: he worked out of the head office, which was located in Canary Wharf. Even better, she'd managed to track down his private residence: a large house in rural Oxfordshire.

All very nice, and if I wasn't mistaken, paid for with the

blood of some of our most vulnerable citizens.

I gave Aunt Lucy a call. It rang out for ages, and I was just beginning to think she wasn't around when she picked up.

"Hello? Jill? Sorry it took me so long to answer. I've got Lil and Lily here. I had to put them both down first."

"Mindy told me that the twins were poorly. How are you coping?"

"Alright, but I'll definitely sleep tonight. I just hope I don't go down with the bug too."

"I'm sorry to trouble you, but is there any way I can get hold of Lester?"

"It's his day off, actually. He's just nipped out to the shops for me — hold on, I think I just heard him come back in. Do you want to speak to him?"

"Yes, please."

Once I'd outlined my plan to Lester, he immediately agreed to help. There wasn't time to travel to London by conventional means, so I magicked myself there, and met Lester outside the office block where SobersCare head office was located.

"Thanks for doing this, Lester."

"No problem. To be honest, I'm glad to get away from the two youngsters for a while."

"They must be hard work?"

"Lucy seems to take it all in her stride, but I find them exhausting. What exactly do you need me to do?"

"Not much, actually. I just want you by my side when I confront Sobers."

"Do you have an appointment to see him?"

"Not exactly. Come on, let's do this."

SobersCare's head office was located on the fifth floor of the building.

If the woman behind reception had smiled, her face would have cracked. "How can I help?"

"We'd like to see Mr Sobers."

She checked the computer screen. "I don't have any appointments for Mr Sobers this afternoon."

"That's a pity." I cast the 'sleep' spell, and she slumped onto the desk. "Lester, follow me." I led the way down the corridor, checking the names on the doors as we went. "Bingo!"

Mark Sobers' suit definitely wasn't off-the-peg; I could have paid my mortgage for a whole year with what it must have cost. And those teeth? So many and so very white.

"Who are you?" He stood up from behind the huge semi-circular desk.

"I'm Jill and this is Lester. Thank you for agreeing to see us."

"I did no such thing. If you haven't left in five seconds, I'll have security throw you out."

"There's no need for that." I sat at one of the chairs next to his desk, and gestured for Lester to sit next to me.

"What do you want?" Sobers demanded.

"I'd like you to hold a press conference to admit that you're responsible for murdering the residents of your care homes."

"What?" He laughed. "Are you insane? Our residents receive the very best in care."

"That may be true, but only for as long as they're alive. And you make sure that isn't very long, by bumping them off before they get the chance to outstay their welcome, don't you?"

"Really?" He laughed. "And how exactly am I supposed to have done that?"

"You scare them to death."

"What nonsense. I'd like you to leave now."

"It takes a particular type of lowlife to do what you do. Can you imagine how an elderly person feels when they wake up to find what they think is the grim reaper at their bedside? They're terrified. But of course you know that. That's the whole idea, isn't it?"

He picked up the phone. "I'm calling security."

"Guess what Lester here does for a living."

"Sorry?"

"His job? Guess what it is."

"I have no idea."

"Tell him, Lester."

"I'm a grim reaper."

"You see, Mark—can I call you Mark? I feel as though we've bonded already. There really are such things as grim reapers, but they don't go around dressed in hooded robes or carry sickles."

"You're mad. Barking mad."

"Not only are grim reapers real, so too are ghosts. And right now, there are a lot of very angry ghosts who would like nothing better than to spend some time with you. Have you ever been haunted, Mark? It can be a very unpleasant experience. You'll never get another good night's sleep."

"Security? This is Mark Sobers on the fifth floor. Can you get someone up here straight away? Thanks." He replaced the receiver. "They'll be here in a few minutes."

"That's okay. We were just leaving, anyway." I stood

up. "But think on it, Mark, the only way to stop the haunting will be to give a press conference and admit your guilt to the nation. I'll be keeping an eye out for it."

After Lester and I had left Sobers' office, I revived the receptionist, and then we both magicked ourselves out of the building before the security men arrived.

"Thanks for that, Lester."

"No problem. Do you really think Sobers will make a full confession on national TV?"

"Right now? Not a chance. But something tells me that by tomorrow morning, he may have had a change of heart."

"I'd better get back to help Lucy."

"Okay, tell her I'll see her soon."

Chapter 21

Just before midnight, I magicked myself to Mark Sobers' mansion where Constance Bowler and several other ghosts were already waiting for me.

"Hi, guys," I greeted them. "This is a great turn out."

"They didn't need any persuading," Constance said.

"I had no idea that Sobers had been responsible for so many deaths."

"This isn't even all of them. A few of them had prior commitments so weren't able to come."

"Have you told them what I'd like them to do?"

"Only briefly. It might be a good idea if you were to run through it with them now."

"Sure." I turned to the assembled ghosts. "Thanks for coming here tonight. You all have one thing in common, and that's that Mark Sobers was responsible for your untimely death."

"He should be strung up!" the old girl at the front of the crowd shouted.

"That's too good for him," the man next to her said.

"We won't be stringing him up, but if everything goes according to plan, we'll shut down his cruel organisation, and put him behind bars for the rest of his miserable life."

"That sounds good to me." The old girl obviously approved. "What do you need us to do?"

"I want you to do to him what he did to you. I want you to give him the scare of his life."

"I have a question, Jill," Constance said. "No one here is attached to Sobers, so he won't actually see anything. Do you think that the drop in temperature and the sense of their presence will be enough to scare him?"

"Probably not. That's why I'm going to cast a spell that will allow you to be visible to him. The spell will only last for a few hours, but hopefully that will be long enough to do the trick."

"Are you going to wait here, Jill?" Constance said.

"No. Once I've cast the spell, there isn't really anything else I can do, and besides, I've barely had any sleep over the last couple of days." I turned to the others. "I'm relying on you lot to scare him witless. Can you do it?"

Their response was emphatic, and left me in no doubt that Sobers was in for the worst night of his life.

By the time I arrived home, Jack was snoring. I joined him in our new bed, and no sooner had my head hit the pillow than I too was fast asleep.

***

"Hey, Lazy Bones." Jack gently shook my shoulder. "I'm just off."

"What time is it?"

"Just turned seven."

I sat up in bed. "How come you're going so early?"

"It's my course. Had you forgotten?"

"I thought you were going tonight?"

"It's the meet and greet this afternoon, so I'm driving there this morning. What time did you get in last night?"

"After midnight. I'm shattered."

"You'll have all weekend to rest up."

"I intend to. This weekend is officially designated: Jill's pamper time."

"I'll see you late on Sunday, then." He gave me a kiss.

"Drive carefully."

I had planned on having just another thirty minutes in bed, but the next thing I knew, I woke up to find it was nine o'clock.

I called Mrs V.

"These are the offices of—"

"Mrs V, it's me."

"Good morning, dear."

Morning. I need you to do something for me. Will you call Sir Arthur Hasbene, and ask him to come to my office today? Any time after ten. Tell him I have some positive news about the missing jewellery."

"I'll get straight on it."

"He'll probably try to insist that I go to Hasbene Hall. If he does, you have to persuade him that the meeting must be at my office."

"Don't worry, dear. I can be very persuasive when I need to be. I'll tell him I have no way of contacting you to rearrange the venue."

"Great, thanks. Call me back when you know what time he's coming over, would you?"

"Will do."

I didn't normally get to watch breakfast TV because either I was in too much of a rush, or Jack was watching TenPin TV. This morning, though, the TV was all mine.

The news was as depressing as always, and I was just about to turn it off when I spotted something on the news ticker on the bottom of the screen:

Business Newsflash: Mark Sobers, CEO of SobersCare, has called an emergency press conference at ten am.

Mrs V rang back.

"Jill, Sir Arthur wasn't very happy, but he's agreed to come in at eleven-thirty."

"Well done. I'll see you just before then."

After making two more calls, I settled down in front of the TV, and waited for the press conference.

On screen, Mark Sobers was standing outside the offices of SobersCare. He looked a shadow of the man I'd met only the day before; he had a haunted look in his eyes.

"I've called this press conference this morning because there's something very important I have to say." He hesitated, took a deep breath, and then in a wavering voice continued, "I am personally responsible for the deaths of many of the residents who entrusted their safety to my organisation. SobersCare is profitable only because of these unforgivable acts. I'm also responsible for the death of Donna Lewis, a reporter who was going to publish an expose of SobersCare. As soon as this press conference has concluded, I intend to hand myself over to the authorities."

After he'd finished speaking, there was a barrage of questions, but he'd obviously said all he intended to say.

The on-the-scene reporter then spoke into the camera, "That is quite the most extraordinary press conference I've ever attended. The implications are obviously dire both for SobersCare and for Mark Sobers himself. We'll bring you more on this story as we get it."

***

"Would you care for a drink, Sir Arthur?"

"No, I'd rather get on with this. I don't know why you had to drag me here, anyway. Surely, we could have done this at Hasbene Hall?"

"I appreciate your coming in. Two more people will be joining us in a moment."

"What? Who?"

"Wait there, please." I walked through to the outer office. "You can go and get them now, Mrs V."

Moments later, she returned with Joanne Carling and Mrs Sykes. I'd had Mrs V ask them to wait down the corridor because I didn't want Sir Arthur to see them on his way in.

"Why are *they* here?" Sir Arthur raged.

"Please take a seat, ladies," I said.

"I demand to know what is going on!" Sir Arthur was on his feet now.

"Please sit down. I asked Joanne and Mrs Sykes to come here so that you can give them what is rightfully theirs."

"I've had quite enough of this." He started towards the door.

"Before you go, perhaps you'd care to explain this?"

He turned around, ready to give me both barrels, but then saw what I was holding.

"Where did you get that?"

"I think you should come and sit down."

Still staring at the Will in my hand, he did as I said.

"According to your late wife's Will, all of her possessions should have gone to her sister. That is, all except for six pieces of jewellery which were bequeathed to Mrs Sykes."

"Geraldine wasn't in her right mind when she wrote

that!" he blustered.

"I'm confident her doctor will testify otherwise. Of course, that will only be necessary if we're forced to take this to the police. I'm sure they'd be interested to know why you deliberately hid the Will."

"I—err—"

"So, what's it to be? Will you give Joanne and Mrs Sykes what is rightfully theirs, or shall I call in the police?"

If looks could kill, I would be six-feet under.

"Alright, alright." He stood up again. "I'll sort it out."

"If you don't, I'll tell the police that you hid the Will. Do I make myself clear?"

"Crystal."

"Good."

"Don't you dare send me a bill for any of your time," he said, and then stormed out of the office.

"Thank you so very much." Mrs Sykes had tears in her eyes. "That money will make all the difference in the world to me."

"Lady Geraldine knew that, which is why she wanted you to have it."

"What I don't understand," Joanne said. "Is how you managed to find the Will."

"A little Gerry told me where it was."

***

"Have you ever considered entering the business woman of the year competition?" Winky jumped onto my desk.

"I assume that's sarcasm?"

"It takes a special skill-set to successfully close a case,

and yet not get paid for it."

"It was the right thing to do."

"You should tweet about it. Hashtag HowToGoBroke."

"Shut up."

My phone rang.

"You should get that." Winky grinned. "It's probably another charity case."

"Hello?"

"Jill, it's Bob Bobb."

"Hi, Bob."

"I just wanted to let you know that your plan worked like a dream."

"That's great. What happened?"

"Driller spiked the drink, just like you said he would."

"Has he been arrested?"

"Yes, and there's even better news. Driller may be a slimeball, but he's no idiot. From what I hear, he's already trying to cut a deal by offering to tell everything he knows about Gillian Happ and the set-up at Mimage. If I was a betting man, I'd wager that this time next week, Mimage will be history."

"That's fantastic news."

"And it's all down to you. Everything King Dollop said about you is true. You'll be sure to send me your bill, won't you?"

"I certainly will."

"See," I turned to Winky. "That was a satisfied, *paying* customer. Hashtag UpYoursWinky."

***

It had been a long week, and I was about to call it a day when Mrs V popped her head around the door.

"Mr and Mrs Banks are here. They wondered if you might spare them a minute?"

"Yes, of course. Send them through."

"Oh, and they have someone else with them." She grinned.

Mr and Mrs Banks were all smiles. So was Annette.

"It's nice to see that you've been reunited. Come and take a seat."

"Annette came home this morning." Christine Banks looked like a woman who had just won the lottery.

"Did you see the press conference, Jill?" Annette said.

"I did."

"Sobers has already been arrested," Gordon chipped in.

"I'm delighted to hear it."

"I rushed back home as soon as I saw the news." Annette turned to her parents. "I feel so bad about putting them through all of this."

"Did you know Sobers was going to do this, Jill?" Gordon said.

"I did pay him a visit yesterday."

"What happened?"

"Let's just say I made him see the error of his ways."

"See, Christine, I told you this was all Jill's doing."

"We can't thank you enough for bringing Annette back to us." Christine wiped away a tear.

"My pleasure. What do you think will happen to the care homes that Sobers owned?"

"I'm not sure," Annette said. "But whoever takes them over, it's sure to be an improvement on what's gone before."

"Annette, do you mind if I ask, have you really split up with Craig or was that just part of the act to throw everyone off the scent?"

"We really have split up; that happened some time ago. But we're still really good friends, and he was the first person I turned to when this blew up. In fact, he was the one who suggested that I go into hiding."

"We'd better not take up any more of your time." Gordon stood up. "We just wanted to come and thank you in person. Do make sure you let us have your bill."

"Hear that Winky? Hashtag MoreCashForJill."

I was halfway down the stairs when who should appear in the doorway but Mindy.

"You only just caught me. I'm on my way home."

"I wanted to let you know that you were right about Gloria. I caught her red-handed, stealing from the till."

"Did she admit she was seeing Miles?"

"Yes, she really believes they're an item, but my guess is that now she's no longer of any use to him, he'll dump her."

"You sacked her, I assume?"

"Of course, but not before I'd made her pay back the money she'd taken. I said if she didn't, I'd call the police." Mindy took three banknotes out of her purse. "This is the money you lent me."

"Thanks."

"No, thank you. You didn't have to believe me, and I wouldn't have blamed you if you hadn't."

**

At long last it was Saturday morning. It had been a hectic couple of weeks, and I was well and truly exhausted. Although I was going to miss Jack, I was looking forward to a totally chilled out weekend topped with plenty of pampering. First stop: the spa.

I was just about to call them to make a booking when my phone rang.

"Jill?"

"Aunt Lucy? Is that you? You sound terrible."

"Lester and I have come down with this horrible flu."

"I'm really sorry to hear that."

"The thing is, we still have Lil and Lily with us."

"Are the twins going to come and get them?"

"They're still laid up too."

"Who's going to look after them, then?"

"That's why I called. I hate to ask, but—"

"Me?"

"That's so very kind."

"I—err—but—"

"I'll get their stuff ready. Thanks ever so."

I stared at the phone in disbelief. This could not be happening.

Twenty minutes later, I had Lil and Lily in my living room.

"Okay, you two. I don't want any trouble from either of you."

They both looked at me with wide eyes and gurgled with joy. Maybe it wasn't going to be so bad after all. I might not be able to go to the spa, but I could still chill out in front of the TV.

"Lil, why are you crying? What's that smell? Lily, don't you start too. Which one of you has made that awful pong?" I sniffed Lil's nappy. "It's you, isn't it?" Wait a minute. I sniffed Lily's. "What is this? Synchronised pooing?"

ALSO BY ADELE ABBOTT

The Witch P.I. Mysteries
(A Candlefield/Washbridge Series)

Witch Is When... (Books #1 to #12)
Witch Is When It All Began
Witch Is When Life Got Complicated
Witch Is When Everything Went Crazy
Witch Is When Things Fell Apart
Witch Is When The Bubble Burst
Witch Is When The Penny Dropped
Witch Is When The Floodgates Opened
Witch Is When The Hammer Fell
Witch Is When My Heart Broke
Witch Is When I Said Goodbye
Witch Is When Stuff Got Serious
Witch Is When All Was Revealed

Witch Is Why... (Books #13 to #24)
Witch Is Why Time Stood Still
Witch is Why The Laughter Stopped
Witch is Why Another Door Opened
Witch is Why Two Became One
Witch is Why The Moon Disappeared
Witch is Why The Wolf Howled
Witch is Why The Music Stopped
Witch is Why A Pin Dropped
Witch is Why The Owl Returned
Witch is Why The Search Began
Witch is Why Promises Were Broken
Witch is Why It Was Over

Witch Is How... (Books #25 to #36)
Witch is How Things Had Changed
Witch is How Berries Tasted Good
Witch is How The Mirror Lied
Witch is How The Tables Turned
Witch is How The Drought Ended
Witch is How The Dice Fell
Witch is How The Biscuits Disappeared
Witch is How Dreams Became Reality
Witch is How Bells Were Saved
Witch is How To Fool Cats
Witch is How To Lose Big
Witch is How Life Changed Forever

Susan Hall Investigates
(A Candlefield/Washbridge Series)
Whoops! Our New Flatmate Is A Human.
Whoops! All The Money Went Missing.
Whoops! Someone Is On Our Case.

Web site: AdeleAbbott.com
Facebook: facebook.com/AdeleAbbottAuthor
Instagram: #adele_abbott_author

Printed in Great Britain
by Amazon